MW00778344

GALWAY'S EDGE

GALWAY'S EDGE

A Jack Taylor Novel

KEN BRUEN

THE MYSTERIOUS PRESS
NEW YORK

GALWAY'S EDGE

Mysterious Press
An Imprint of Penzler Publishers
58 Warren Street
New York, N.Y. 10007

Copyright © 2025 by Ken Bruen

First Mysterious Press edition

Interior design by Maria Fernandez

Library of Congress Control Number: 2024918809

ISBN: 978-1-61316-600-0
eBook ISBN: 978-1-61316-601-7

10 9 8 7 6 5 4 3 2 1

Printed in the United States of America
Distributed by W. W. Norton & Company

For

Mark O'Connor

and

Lucy

For Declan and Annette Coyle

and

their amazing Alexander.

Warmest wishes to to you and your family.

Ken

"I'm sorry I called you an
arsehole.
I thought
You already knew."

Edge.

In its various manifestations, edge could be interpreted in many Irish ways, i.e., nonlogical. As shown below.

Ireland lies on the edge of Europe.

Edge describes a person with a knife-edge personality.

Edge is an urban myth of a vigilante group.

Having the edge, meaning the inside stuff on a situation.

The cutting edge implies the sharp knowledge denied to most.

Edge came to mean an absolute living nightmare in the dying days of 2022.

1

A notorious paedophile, named Cleon, managed to avoid prosecution despite appalling acts. He boasted to his abuser's circle.

"I'm fucking bulletproof."

Edge stepped in.

Edge were founded when the twelve tribes ruled Galway. Thus began a cabal who effectively ruled the city, stepping in when normal issues needed to be resolved. They discovered early that secrecy and subterfuge were powerful tools. As a person in the city rose in the community, they were approached by Edge to join. Rumours were their stock in trade. Gathering information, collecting sordid acts, wielding power from a city that didn't know that they were.

By stealth and money, they managed to exist as a rumour masquerading as a fact.

The paedophile was found burned to a crisp in his brand-new Audi, strapped in the driver's seat, the burnt remnants of toys scattered all over his stinking corpse.

Most days I went to sit at the bedside of a man in a coma; he was allegedly the predator who had been attacking nuns.

I had entered a pact with a group called Edge, they promised to deliver him to me.

But

I had to pledge a favour they might ask in the future.

When Raftery, the coma man, was finally presented to me, I swung a hurly at his head, didn't kill him but flung him into this state.

I sat by his bed, wating for him to wake and then what?

Then we'd see.

I had been bequeathed a dog by an ex-nun named Sheila Winston; she, too, had become a Raftery victim.

The dog was a shih tzu named Trip. The dog and I took quite a wedge of time before we settled into each other's world. But he was now an integral part of mine. He was a daily shot of unadulterated joy, and I loved him to bits.

Did he love me? Not so much. But I fed him, walked him (a lot), and he seemed resigned to his fate.

Into my life, too, had come a fine woman named Rachel. It was she who acted as a conduit to Edge, but we were circling the prospect of becoming an item.

I didn't have to walk her or indeed feed her.

Least not yet.

2

Saturday, 5 November 2022.
The state of the world.

Ireland had to cap the number of refugees from Ukraine as we had
literally no place to house them anymore. Two hundred were already
sleeping in the airport!

Nancy Pelosi's husband, eighty-two years old, was the subject of a violent assault in his home. The attacker beat him with a hammer, screaming,

"Where's Nancy?"

This was the war cry when the White House was near overrun by
Trump zealots.

In the cervical cancer scandal in Ireland, another of the beautiful
women who had been misdiagnosed died at the age of thirty-two. She
left behind two gorgeous wee girls.

The country was battered by storms and many homes were flooded.

Inflation was out of control and fuel, gas, power were nigh ten times the amounts before the Ukraine war.

I managed to take Trip for a ferocious wind-strewn walk and he relished the battle to stay upright against the gales.

I was fortified by a hot Jameson and told myself,

"This is life on the edge."

During my befuddled life, I've had a deck of priests splatter over my existence.

Two of the more nefarious are dead.

I'm not even going to try to figure why dead priests litter my landscape.

And nuns?

Phew-oh.

I was home in my apartment, drenched after an abortive attempt to wash Trip in the bath.

I swear to God, Trip loved showering me with bathwater and suds.

At least he was clean if damp, like the country used to be.

I was wearing a T-shirt with The Saw Doctors on the front, very faded 501s, and a pair of broken-in Crocs.

Crocs!

Making a huge comeback, which shows that ugly does indeed have its day.

I was kind of barefoot and kind of fancy-free.

The doorbell zinged, I opened it to the fattest priest I've ever seen and tall with it.

At the hope of being cancelled, I say *fat* as adjectives like

Obese

Rotund

Piggy

Deserve to be cancelled.

He wheezed,

"Jack Taylor?"

I said 'twas me.

He surveyed me, my bare feet, worn gear, said,

"I'm Father Richard, special envoy to the Archdiocese of Galway, Tuam, and Athenry. The powers that be decreed I should contact you as you have been of considerable assistance to Mother Church, not to mention, somewhat controversial. May I come in?"

The devil was in me to accuse,

"Think you'll fit?"

But I let that slide, I can do diplomacy, if rarely.

He lumbered in, his black suit bulging in all the hard places.

Trip ran to him, wagging his tail furiously. The little bastard.

Richard said,

"Dogs love me."

Huge point in his favour. He swooped Trip who smothered his face with licks, and they collapsed on the couch.

I said,

"I'm afraid of folk who are afraid of dogs."

He liked that.

His face was large with the purple patches of the habitual drinker, I know my drinkers. He had one of those odd cupid mouths that recall the tag,

"Prissy."

But his eyes, big blue orbs that shone with good nature. I asked,

"Might I wet your whistle?"

I might.

And did.

I poured a large, asked,

"Ice?"

He snapped.

"Don't be ridiculous."

A man of my tribe.

Plus, I didn't have ice.

Save for the chip in my soul.

He held the heavy Galway glass tumbler of Jay up to the light, asked,

"Is there a grander sight?"

I said,

"The next one."

He laughed out loud, his massive bulk shaking the couch and the dog. I asked,

"Why are you here?"

He took a sizable wallop of the Jay, said,

"We have become aware of a group named Edge who are anti-Catholic."

I gave a bitter laugh, said,

"Like most of the country."

He let that go, continued,

"Among this group it is rumoured they have a priest."

I said,

"That's the clergy for you, stuck in every pie."

He shook his head, said,

"Nevertheless, we need you to locate this individual and dissuade him of his activities."

He added quickly,

"We will of course recompense you for your time."

I let out my breath, asked,

"What's his name and where does he hang?"

"Kevin Whelan, he is parish priest at St. Joseph's."

I asked,

"Am I allowed to bring my hurly?"

He was genuinely at a loss, asked,

"Why?"

I said drily,

"To dissuade him."

" 'We are not like them,' said Spiridon, as his brother fell into step beside him. 'And we will never be.'

'Small details will betray us,' said Radovan.

'No,' said Spiridon, "only small men.' "

—John Connolly

The Nameless Ones

3

As Father Richard prepared to leave, he handed me an envelope, said,

"For expenses."

I took it.

"I'll buy some treat for the dog."

Richard looked at me, asked,

"Aren't you going to count it?"

I gave him my best smile.

"You're a priest, isn't trust in your brief?"

His eyes scanned the apartment and I saw his gaze land on a particular volume, he asked,

"Is that Declan's book, *The Green Platform*?"

I nodded and he asked,

"Might I borrow it?"

I took the book, said,

"Beware the red platform."

He gave a rueful smile.

"Alas, I have some work in that direction."

I said,

"Me too."

And he was gone, saying he'd be in touch. I ventured,

"I'll try to contain my excitement."

The dog seemed to miss him.

Being overweight,

Is a constant cross,

You don't get days off,

Where you might think you're not so heavy

You go,

Did I lose a few pounds?

You didn't.

You avoid mirrors,

For a shard of measured relief.

Richard suffered daily from his condition.

The shame

The heart worry,

His actual appearance

Jibes from the public.

Clothes that fit,

He was forty-five years of age, felt eighty, looked sixty-eight, and prayed to God,

"Let me be thin."

But to date added

"But not yet."

He loved his food and it'd be debatable if food loved him but, in every sense, it devoured him. He had spent five years as a troubleshooter in the Vatican and to survive that predatory state, you needed all the weight you could throw.

You needed edge.

And he had that in spades.

The pope had once referred to him as an ecclesiastical barracuda.

His appearance led people to believe he was a pushover.

Big mistake.

Richard had been summoned to the inner sanctums. That meant one of three things:

You were fired.

You were promoted (highly unlikely).

There was a dirty job coming down the papal pike.

It was the third.

Richard was ushered into a lavish room, ornate furnishings and Rembrandt on the wall. Sitting behind a massive oak desk was the scourge of the Vatican.

Monsignor Benedict.

You heard rumours of his ruthlessness in every corner of the state. He was a small man, with a goatee, nigh completely bald, a body disguised in a habit and then you got to his eyes.

Phew-oh.

As Robert Shaw described a shark's eyes in *Jaws*, he had the eyes of a doll.

A very malignant one.

He indicated that Richard should take the hard Louis Quinze chair in front of his desk, sneered,

"If you can fit into it, that is."

Richard did fit into the chair but not without wheezing and panting. Benedict flourished a gold Montblanc pen, pointed it at Richard, asked,

"You'll have heard of Father Sheehy's fuckup."

That priest was eighty years of age and had been loaned from the US to fill in for a sick priest. He gave a sermon that said,

*There are only men and women. Trans, LGBTQ, etc. were
Sins.*

He proceeded to lash sinners and delivered a ferocious homily that fire
and brimstone doesn't even come close to describing. Our gay prime
minister was of course hugely irate, and the government lined up to
condemn him.

He could have given a flying fuck, told them all he was simply
quoting the Bible.

Richard admired him greatly.

Benedict not so much.

He said,

"You're going to Ireland to shut him down and to deal with Kevin
Whelan."

Benedict pressed a button on the desk and minutes later a Swiss
Guard appeared with a tray holding two glasses.

He gently put them on the desk and skedaddled. Benedict asked,

"Is Black Bush to your liking?"

Richard wanted to shake the whole tone of Benedict's spiel, asked,

"Isn't that the whiskey of the Protestants?"

Benedict scowled, snapped,

"Don't be a cunt, drink up."

The foul language was, Richard knew, designed to intimidate.

He took a large gulp from his glass, waited, then belched loudly. He
could be crude his own self.

It amused Benedict who said,

"Here's a wee history lesson for you, tubby. In every major city is a group of people called, loosely, Edge. They function in the shadows, step in when other solutions are lost. Papal funds have been sent their way in the past. Now this Kevin Whelan is far too enmeshed in the Galway branch and your assignment, should you choose to accept it . . ."

He paused, tittered at his *Mission Impossible* joke, continued,

"Your task is to silence this idiot."

Richard took a breath, asked,

"Silence?"

Benedict waved a hand dismissively, said,

"You're a man of heft, bring your weight to the problem, now fuck off, your flight to Ireland is at seven this evening."

Richard got painfully to his feet, asked,

"If I decline the mission?"

Benedict laughed, said,

"We know about Leona, your concubine,

"Bit of fluff

"Bit on the side

"Mistress,

"And you annoy me, she finds herself on the street, clear?"

Very.

Richard did indeed have a girlfriend, but women and the clergy were tolerated, any scandal preferable to rumours of child abuse.

He said,

"Thanks for the drink."

Benedict laughed, said,

"Consider it a poisoned chalice."

Richard's flight was a trial. Due to his girth, he had to book two seats but as it was on the Vatican's dime, who gave a toss. The air hostess—if you can still call them such—whispered,

"We have a vacancy in first class, would you like that?"

Would he?

Fuck!

Yes.

Now here was a seat that fit.

He settled in and got a welcoming glass of champagne.

One could get used to such.

He was about to read the *Financial Times* when the man in the seat opposite asked,

"You're thinking you recognize me?"

Richard thought absolutely nothing about him, save he was already annoying.

The man ploughed on. He was maybe fifty, dressed in an Armani suit, with a deep tan, grey coiffed hair, and nasty eyes.

Richard braced himself as the plane took off, the man chuckled, said,

"Nervous flyer, huh?"

As the flight levelled out, the hostess came with a tray of cocktails. The man took two; Richard settled for what looked like a frozen margarita. The man downed one drink, asked,

"So, you recognize me?"

Richard, feeling the tequila hit, said,

"No."

The man was unruffled, he was of the type,

I will be heard and now!

He said,

"You're familiar with the megahit show, *Succession*?"

Richard let the booze ease him on down, tried,

"I saw the first series."

He didn't.

The man grimaced, nigh spat,

"You haven't seen the second and third ones?"

Like serious sins?

Richard said,

"I have them, just not the time."

Out came the man's hand. He barked,

"Thomas T. McKenna, I was big in the second series."

Then he tittered, amended,

"Whoa, didn't mean anything by"

Pause.

"Big."

The waitress came with menus and more booze. Richard got out the complimentary eye mask, said,

"I'm going to rest now."

Thomas T. was horrified, accused,

"You're not going to eat?"

Richard said,

"I'm on a diet."

Thomas T. snarled,

"It ain't working, pal."

Later, Richard woke after a disturbing dream about his woman Leona. She was a true peasant feisty fireball from Naples, she grew up in the infamous Gomorrah. In the dream she was being ridden by Benedict, who was grinning like a mini-Satan.

Thomas T. said,

"You're sweating like a stuck pig there, buddy."

Richard put his headphones on, checked the movie menu.

He chose *The Whale*.

Starring Brendan Fraser, playing a man who weighed forty-three stone and the trials and tribulations of his life. Thomas T., who'd watched the same movie, said,

"You could be twins."

Brendan Fraser had once been the golden boy of Hollywood, hits like

George of the Jungle,

The Mummy

Made him the star of a particular Los Angeles moment then it all went down the golden toilet and he disappeared. This return to the screen got him a standing ovation in Cannes and an Oscar possibility.

Richard wiped tears from his eyes, closely monitored by the vigilant Thomas T. who asked,

"Hey buddy, I never asked, what's your line of work?"

He paused,

Added,

"Something heavy, eh?"

Richard rarely wore the clerical collar; it was, combined with his weight, like a target on his ample back. He decided to go with the truth, maybe shut this arsehole up.

Bad idea.

He said,

"I'm a priest."

Before Thomas T. could respond, the hostess arrived with more champagne and said they would be landing within the hour. When Richard thanked her, she leant over, said,

"God bless you, Padre."

Thomas T. snickered and Richard summoned him to move closer. Which Thomas T. did eagerly.

Richard jabbed the flat of his hand into the stomach of Thomas T. This move was a speciality of the women of Naples. Leona had taught it to Richard. He said to Thomas T.,

"That is the first of five blows I can administer, so you have one question to answer—are you going to shut your mouth?"

Thomas T., unable to speak, nodded yes. Richard sat back, said,

"Consider it as a succession of blows you avoided, but now your season is over, your option has not been renewed."

When the plane landed, Richard was on his way out when the hostess whispered,

"You're my hero."

Sometimes, the fat guy does sing.

The Razor's Edge
W. Somerset Maugham

4

The five,

Who

Comprise

The

Edge

In

Galway.

The Five

1. Lukas Ortiz (literary agent)

2. Philomena Dunphy (real estate mogul)

3. P. J. Duggan (billionaire)

4. Martin de Breen (best-selling author)

5. Kevin Whelan (priest)

I got the list from my old drinking mate in the Guards. He looked haggard.

Would I say that to my buddy?

I said,

"You look haggard."

We were on our second pint, and he put his glass down, said,

"That's a bollix of a thing to say,"

Is it?

He said,

"Getting that list was nigh impossible; in the Force, we know about them, well some of their activities, I mean who's not going to like a crew who rid the city of vermin, plus the simple fact that those five are seriously fucking rich. But it is not mentioned lest they decide to deal with Guards. You owe me big time and instead of your undying gratitude, I need cash, my wife is divorcing me and I'm hurting for cash money."

The devil was in me, and I asked,

"Why not lean on one of Edge?"

He signalled for another round,

"Put some Jameson on point."

Then to me,

"What's your interest?"

I said,

"The priest; I'm being paid to tell him to cease and desist, whatever he's at."

The drinks came and I took out my wallet. Owen saw a rash of notes, heavy wedge, he said,

"I'll be having that."

I gave it to him and asked,

"Who should I seek out first?"

He raised his Jay, clinked my glass, cheered,

"Sláinte."

I answered,

"Leat féin."

He gave me a hard look, asked,

"Who is employing you to find the priest?"

I told the truth, said,

"The Vatican."

He shot back,

"Fuck off."

He told me to go after the woman first, get a sense of Edge.

Added,

"She's a ball-breaker, lives in Water Lane and if you ask a resident which house's hers, they'll point out the row of houses on the left and tell you, all of them."

I finished my pint, said,

"Thanks for the info, I'm going to see her now while the booze still sings in my blood, plus you've taken my money."

He said,

"Bill the Vatican."

He had managed to get a mobile number for her, said,

"Those cost extra."

I tried,

"I'm good for it, see you next time."

He shook his head,

"You were never good for it."

"Vicky Phelan died today.

A fighter who forced the forces that be that she and 210 women

Were lied to about

The tests for cervical cancer,

Effectively condemning them to die.

She refused to sign an NDA when they agreed to pay her

So her children would be cared for.

She was only forty-eight.

The country loved this down-to-earth woman and

National outpourings of grief enveloped the nation."

5

I took Trip for a run in Eyre Square, and with delight watched him socialise with other dogs.

I had my mobile, rang the Dunphy lady.

Told her who I was and could I talk with her about Edge.

She said,

"Vicky Phelan died this morning so you—"

Pause.

"—can fuck off."

Okay.

The dog was having such a wild time, I decided to let him run longer. There was a drinking school lurking under the nearby trees and staring in my direction. One was elected and ambled toward me. He had the hardened look of street, could be thirty or fifty. Dressed in a forlorn coat of the former Irish army, a heavy green number, he was tall but stooped, had a limp and a full head of wiry grey hair. There was a slight tremor in his gait, and I could see him fix his smile to be beseeching but with a hint of fuck you.

He said,

"A good day to you sir."

I said,

"That's a bad intro, smacks of condescension."

He smiled, missing most of his top row teeth, and produced a crushed pack of Major, the coffin nails. He offered the pack, asked,

"Fancy a tote?"

Trip came bounding to me, gave the man a hard look, then sat beside me.

The man produced one of those large kitchen boxes of matches, managed to light a cig, said,

"That's a fine dog, where would a fella find such a treasure?"

His accent mutated into a semi–Globe Theatre tone, and I swear either that or the cig wrought the change. There was now a mocking slant to his posture.

I don't do mockery, shot back,

"A nun bequeathed him."

He didn't buy this, echoed,

"A nun, what kind of nun has a dog like that?"

I said,

"A dead one."

He did a show tremor, went,

"Bejaysus."

I was waiting for the hit and come it did, he asked,

"Might a chap trouble you for the price of a cup of tea?"

I gave him a twenty, shocking him, he said,

"That's a tidy sum; God and His Holy Mother mind you."

I put the lead on Trip, rose to go, he asked,

"And who might you be, sir?"

I sighed, said,

"Someone who knows dead nuns."

Joe Peet was the driving force of the Galway rugby team. Guy like that, he can do no wrong, well, no wrong he was ever going to be held accountable for.

He liked to kick the shit out of his wife and used a black thick leather belt.

But then he overstepped the mark and beat her so badly she was unconscious in the hospital, her face literally broken.

He was arrested.

A short trial was always going to be about his prowess at sport.

He was given a suspended sentence and the judge commended his remorse and deep regret.

One week later, he was found on the rugby pitch. He had been beaten to death.

His face was literally broken and his belt, the thick leather one, stuffed in his mouth.

Edge had spoken.

18 November 2022

Russia seems on
The EDGE
Of launching missiles
Across
Ukraine.

6

I found Father Kevin Whelan, using all my detection skills.

I went to St. Patrick's Church, where he was listed as the parish priest.

Knocked on the door of his adjoining house, a fine one, no expense spared on the outside. The doorbell played "Amazing Grace."

Irony, eh?

Big kidders, huh.

A priest answered.

Dressed in a black shirt, faded jeans, but with a crease.

Ugh.

Soft moccasins with tassels, kind of mixed message, like,

"I'm cool but an ejit."

I asked,

"Father Whelan?"

"Yes, who's asking?"

I chose to fuck with him a bit, priests have fucked with us long enough.

I said,

"The Vatican."

He invited me in, large sitting room, log-blazing fire, soft furnishings, and, surely not, a Jack Yeats painting.

He indicated a rocking chair, asked,

"A drink?"

I said in mock-cheery tone,

"That would be spiffing."

"I know who you are, the town dipso, Taylor, so I guess a Jameson, no ice?"

And why not?

He served up tumblers of Jay on a silver tray, fucking with me.

Good.

Bring it on, priest.

I rocked on the chair, enjoying the soft motion.

He settled down in an easy chair with a copy of *The Wreck of The Deutschland*, a study of Gerald Manley Hopkins, he clocked my look, asked,

"You interested in that?"

I said,

"Dead nuns follow me."

(Five nuns had drowned in the wreck.)

He chuckled, offered,

"How odd."

He held up his glass, cheered,

"Here's to dead nuns."

I didn't rise to this, went,

"Whatever you are at, none of my business, but the Vatican wants you to stop."

He laughed out loud, said,

"How fucking dramatic."

I loved the swearing, said,

"You're part of Edge."

Got him.

He stood up, spluttered,

"Time for you to hit the road, pal."

I stayed sitting, answered,

"When I finish my drink."

He muttered,

"Fuckers."

Then I drank it in one, stood, said,

"It was close to a pleasure."

He sneered, with,

"Now your errand is done, you can go back to being a drunk."

"Back? Call me alarmist, but I'd watch your own *back*!"

I was halfway down the church lane when I realised the heavy glass tumbler was still clutched in my hand. I drained the remnants. God, it tasted fine.

I considered bringing it home, adding it as a slight trophy to the collection of oddments from an odd time.

Then I thought,

"Fuck it."

Threw it hard and fast into the tiny graveyard there where the Dean is buried. Might it amuse him to know the new hotel in Bohermore was named the Dean.

Probably not.

The next day,
November 19,
Father Kevin Whelan
Was found
Hanging from a tree
In his backyard.
The letter E was written in the dirt
Beneath his slippered feet.
The slippers, like those of the pope, were by
Gucci.

7

I was coming out of the shower, grabbing a towel, when an almighty thud hit the front door. Pulling on a tee and jeans, I went barefoot to the door.

Opened it to an irate Father Richard, all twenty stone of him. He stormed in, muttering obscenities. I heard,

"What the hell were you thinking?"

He flopped down on the couch and the dog jumped nimbly on his lap. He didn't seem to mind, glared at me, snarled.

"I need strong coffee, lots of sugar, and biscuits too."

I took a deep breath, said,

"Couple of things, you forgot to say please, you stormed in without invite, and I don't do biscuits."

He rubbed the dog behind its ears, near spat,

"You were supposed to warn Father Whelan off, not kill him, I mean, how extreme did you think you had to be?"

"He's dead?"

Jesus.

He asked,

"You don't know?"

I said,

"Take a wild fat guess."

He settled back of the couch, said,

"He was found hanged in his garden."

I was shocked, lost for words.

Richard asked,

"You went to see him?"

"Yes, I told him it would be in his best interest to cease and desist."

"And?"

"He threw me out."

Richard nearly laughed but pushed it down.

"It has to be Edge."

I was puzzled.

"Why would they kill one of their own?"

He asked,

"Where are we on that coffee?"

I went to the kitchen, brewed some seriously strong coffee, checked the shelf with the dog's treats, one packet looked like yer regular variety, so I put six on a plate, brought them out, set them on the small table beside him.

The dog, who'd been dozing, perked up, looked at me as if,

"Hey, arsehole, those are mine."

Richard took one, dipped it in the coffee, slurped noisily, managed,

"Good choice."

Right.

He asked,

"Mind if I give one to Trip?"

I minded not a whit.

That very sentence smacked of received English. I'd need to watch that.

I asked,

"So, who killed the priest?"

Now that was an Agatha Christie vibe.

He said,

"Edge."

Fuck.

He had finished the biscuits, wiped his mouth, said,

"The priest was, as you laymen call, a kiddie fiddler and due to be prosecuted; we suspect he was trading Edge for clemency. Edge can't have that."

I was stunned, managed,

"You're part of a crew who kill priests."

He waved a thick finger at me.

"Oh no, I'm the messenger."

I snapped,

"Some fucking messenger you are."

He put the dog down, struggled to his feet,

"Your services are no longer required."

I stared, then snarled.

"That's what you think."

"Oh, what a world

That has

Such assholes

In it."

　　—Graffiti on the wall of the nun's convent

8

I decided I'd track some of the names that made Edge.

Philomena Dunphy had already blown me off but that just made it interesting. She was listed as a real estate agent, a partner in Donnellan and Joyce, so I rang them, was told she was showing a house on Threadneedle Road that afternoon.

Dress to impress.

Resurrected my black suit, bought from Oxfam for thirty euro. The jacket sleeves were too long but I could roll them up, go for that mellow biz vibe, the waist was wide, so a thick black belt, keep it dark.

A blue shirt with a tie I stole from a Rotarian, and I was good to go house hunting. My Doc Martens screamed a little out there, but you risk a touch of flair.

When I got to the house for sale, there were quite a bunch of people already viewing.

Dunphy was easy to spot.

A small blond, dressed in blue power suit, nigh killer heels. A face that should have been pretty but missed by some shade of rage.

Fine, I can do rage.

I approached her and she gave me the real-estate smile, all charm, no warmth. She asked,

"Are you looking for single occupancy or family home?"

I smiled, said,

"I'm looking for you."

A beat.

Then she said,

"You've found me, who are you?"

I put out my hand, which she ignored.

I said,

"I'm Jack Taylor."

Took her a few seconds.

"Wait a minute, you're the arsehole who keeps phoning me."

I gave her my version of the real-estate smile, all teeth, no feeling. I asked,

"If I could just have a few minutes of your time?"

She looked around, seeking some help.

There wasn't.

She took a deep breath, said,

"You have two minutes, what do you want?"

"Edge, can you tell me about it."

Shocked her, but she rallied.

"Like in U2?"

"I get that tired line a lot. You might be interested to know I was with Father Whelan hours before he was hanged."

I could see her weighing how much I knew; she said,

"Then you need to talk to the Guards."

Turned on her heel, moved to a couple examining the kitchen. I followed.

She whirled round, said in a low lethal tone,

"I know one thing for sure, shitheads who go nosing in Edge business tend to get hung up."

I tried,

"Father Richard told me about you."

"What is it with you and priests?"

I said,

"They find me a comfort."

She scoffed,

"I very much doubt you have ever been a comfort to anyone."

I gave her a sad face, a blend of naivete and guile, said,

"That's harsh, no wonder you succeed in real estate."

She shook her head.

"I think we're finished here, fella."

I began to move away, said,

"Oh, you'll be seeing me, after I contact the remaining crew of Edge."

"That would be extremely foolish."

I laughed.

"It's what I do best, foolish."

"Getting even
Brings a mannered relief.
But pushing the Edge further
Into the realm of hard-core
Revenge
Is a rush of
Potent power."

9

I was sitting on a bench in Claddagh, Trip was watching the swans with a guarded interest. I was feeding them with the right food, you had to be careful what you gave them as previously, the random bread had erased the waterproofing on these beautiful birds.

On the seat beside me was the new book from Sara Gran.

The Book of the Most Precious Substance.

It was a blend of thriller, eroticism, magic, books, writing, and was just sensational. It was also raunchy as hell, like a banshee in heat. The night before had unleashed biblical rain and Sara's book seemed to be nomadistic.

The streets were washed clean and, thank God, Quay Street hadn't been flooded. Now the sun was peeking through, and temperatures were hitting ten degrees.

My Garda all-weather coat beside me on the bench, Trip hopped up, snuggling himself on it. It gave him some form of comfort; I knew the feeling.

The Garda Communications gang wrote to me periodically asking that I return the coat.

Like fuck.

I heard my name being called and turned to see Brid.

A traveller, shaman, faith healer, and long-standing friend. It was rumoured she'd known Nora Barnacle, Joyce's wife. Like a lot of stories in Galway, it was long on detail and scarce of veracity.

She was dressed in a Connemara shawl, long cotton dress like an escapee from *Little House on the Prairie*, and, incongruously, ballet shoes.

Go figure.

She greeted,

"A cara álainn" (*Beautiful friend*).

As if.

I motioned her to sit beside me, which she did. The dog wagged his tail, he was a fine judge of character.

She asked,

"Madra Nua?" (*New dog?*)

I said,

"It belonged to an ex-nun who died."

Brid blessed herself, rubbed Trip's head.

She had an enormous bag under the shawl, the names of the famine ships were printed on it. She rummaged in it, took out the makings of a cigarette,

Virginia tobacco,

Silver Zippo,

Cig papers.

Delicately, she rolled a perfect tote, handed it to me, flicked the Zippo, that solid clunk is one of my favourite sounds.

She then rolled another, lit up, said,

"A lot of people are going to die."

No argument there.

She continued,

"Bí cúramach." (*Be careful.*)

Careful wasn't really in my gene pool but I said,

"I will."

We sat in a contented silence, then she stood up, I passed a bundle of notes to her, she said,

"You don't need to give me charity."

I said,

"That's not charity, that's grá" (*love*).

She liked that a lot, leaned in, gave me a Galway hug, which is close, and warmth infused. She smelt of patchouli, turf fire, baby powder, and, mostly, compassion.

She rubbed the dog's head and got a furious tail wag.

I watched her walk along the Claddagh pier and two young men were approaching her, one of them spat at her. She took no notice.

I did.

I said to Trip,

"Stay."

As I moved toward the men, they realised I was coming for them and moved apart to engage me. Reaching the first, I said,

"Your nose is broken."

He laughed, mocked,

"No, it isn't."

I headbutted him, the nose broke easily, I turned to the other who whined,

"Wasn't me, I did nothing."

I kicked him in the balls.

As I collected the dog and my coat, I looked back at two gobshites I'd hammered, muttered,

"Whatever I've lost, and God knows I've lost a ferocious amount, I still have edge."

Argue that.

1 December 2022.

Did you know that?
Today
The whole world
Is the same age.
This happens every one thousand years.
Your age and your year of birth,
Every person=2022.

10

P. J. Duggan, the billionaire, one the five names on the list of Edge, was found in his penthouse, stabbed to death. There were more than fifty wounds all over his body.

I was at home, the dog asleep in front of the telly, *The Simpsons* playing quietly. Trip had a thing for Santa's Little Helper.

A pounding on the door, which had the dog on its feet, growling full. I pulled the door open to Father Richard. I snarled,

"You woke the fucking dog."

He asked,

"Is that a metaphor?"

I had to dial it back not to smack him in the mouth, but in my experience no good comes of beating the clergy, they keep coming back.

I stepped aside and he lumbered in, he was dressed in what they call clergy casual.

Chinos

Button-down shirts

Black slip-ons (with yes, those awful tassels)

And of course, the inevitable black raincoat.

The dog changed gear, began to wag his tail, Richard flopped down on the sofa, wheezed,

"I need strong coffee and put a stick in it." (Meaning Jameson.)

"Why don't you just move in, you sure seem at home."

He gave me a look, then,

"Ah Jack, we'd make strange bedfellows."

I shuddered at the prospect.

I made the coffee, put the Jay in, handed him it in a mug that had the logo.

"I'm a gas."

Quiet.

He told me about the murder of P. J. Duggan, emphasised the ferocity of the attack. I said,

"Sounds personal."

He was wrestling with some dilemma, and I said,

"Spit it out."

He drained the coffee.

"Edge has mostly been a force for good, but lately, its members seem to have drifted off into matters personal, neglecting their purpose. The Vatican feels they are now more of a threat than a help. They crossed a man named Benson; do you know of him?"

"No."

Richard pondered more, decided.

"He is an Englishman, made a killing in hedge funds, they call him *Benson and Hedges*."

I muttered,

"Cute."

Richard was all serious now.

"Benson seems to have a notion to erase Edge."

I asked,

"Erase—like what? Spell it out."

His head was down, he said,

"Like stab a man fifty times; his personality would definitely fall on the side of overkill."

Phew-oh.

"Then Edge is bad fucked."

Richard said,

"We can't allow that and worse, Benson is a Protestant."

I nearly laughed.

"Oh, come on, this shite has nowt to do with religion, you can't play the hackney Catholic card, next you'll add that he is a Brit."

He nodded yes.

Fucksakes.

I stood up, indicating time was up.

He said,

"This is where you come in."

What?

I said,

"Ah no, I did the job you paid for, I want no more of this whole insane shindig."

"The Vatican would smile on you."

I snarled.

"That's like an ecclesiastical curse, maybe the pope will send me rosary beads."

A petrol station had exploded in a small village and twelve local people lost their lives. The pope had sent them twelve rosary beads.

Richard was on his feet, swaying slightly, tried,

"We only want you to talk to him, persuade him to back off, look, we'll pay you double the amount of before."

"Nothing will change my mind."

He was heading for the door, rubbing the dog.

"Oh, I think there is one thing that might convince you."

He had a small smile that was circling a smirk. I said,

"Go on, give it your best shot."

He said quietly,

"Rachel is next."

For the second time, I went to the movies; for two hours, I was free of the world. I went to see *Bones and All*.

Wow.

Horror with a whole new twist. The lead actor, Timothée Chalamet.

Was like a young Johnny Depp, the cheekbones, punk attitude. Featured the famed Shakespeare actor Mark Rylance. Two hours and twenty minutes later, it was a movie of deep compassion, with absolute shocks throughout.

I came out in a kind of daze, yearning—for what? Someone to see it with?

I had asked Rachel, she answered,

"I don't really do cinema."

What does that even mean?

I asked,

"What does that even mean?"

She sighed.

"With Ukraine, climate change, the increase in fuel, energy, power, how can anyone *go to the movies*?"

Fuck me.

I said,

"A superficial bollix who doesn't give a toss."

And I cut the call off.

I headed for Garavan's, time for some serious Jameson, the amount a superficial bastard might drink.

"The edge
Of despair
Is only slightly
Removed
From utter surrender.
The very next step
Is a time bomb waiting
To obliterate you."

Edge of the nation.

Christine McVie of Fleetwood Mac died at the age of seventy-nine. For sixteen years, she had lived reclusively in a mansion in Kent. The album Rumours, *recorded in a storm of cocaine, remains one of the best-selling albums of all time. They said if you laid Peter Green's coke used in a single line, it would be seven miles long.*

The first five days of December were an Indian summer.

Ukraine continued to undergo ferocious bombing of civilian targets.

Inflation continued to rise alarmingly. Fuel, gas, power were like wild horses.

The World Cup continued to be mired in controversy. Down to the last sixteen and gone home already were

Argentina

Uruguay

Belgium

The United States.

Meghan and Harry on the verge of releasing their documentary, which, if the trailer was any indication, showed Kate Middleton in a series of bad-tempered, scowling poses. Meghan, of course, seems to have spent the show weeping. In America, the sheen hadn't yet worn off this scheming couple.

In the UK, they were vilified for their betrayal of all things royal.

A former badminton star aged thirty-five was jailed for eight years for paying mothers to provide him with pictures of their very young children; one mother was sentenced to three years in jail.

In the North Wall in Dublin, four hundred male refugees were literally dumped on the small area. Protests were infiltrated by right-wing groups with a whole separate agenda.

11

It wasn't difficult to find Benson. Google provided me with the facts.

Married. With two kids. Literally an empire built on dodgy hedge funds. Google didn't say dodgy of course, but they didn't dismiss it either. He was fifty-eight years of age and had been given Freedom of the City the year before.

Photos showed a bull of a man, close-cropped hair, and closer-cropped eyes.

Even in photos, a power enshrouded him. He played golf regularly with the city elite. I was about to take a swing of my own.

His main office was a massive affair, all glass front beside the Skeffington Arms. Along the front was carved in bronze,

"Benson."

As if that was all you needed to know. Maybe it was.

I had dressed in my second Oxfam outfit, a crisp white suit, a tie, loosened of course, to show I didn't take the suit seriously. The suit certainly didn't take me seriously, it hung on the sleeves and legs. I did a spit and polish on my Doc Martens and was good to go.

I breezed into the main reception area, approaching a lady, busy at a massive desk that looked like it came from mission control. Took her a time to look up, when she did her face suggested that I didn't know the meaning of "tradesman entrance." She asked in an icy tone,

"Yes?"

Clipped, hostile.

"I'm here to see Mr. Benson, or just Benson, if that's how you play."

She allowed a small malignant smile.

"Do you have an appointment?"

I said I didn't and in a triumphant tone, she said,

"Then you're wasting my time."

Her head down again.

I waited until she looked up.

"Was there something else?"

"Tell Benny I'm here on Vatican business."

She bit down on a reply, made a call, listened, then said,

"Mr. Benson will see you now."

I was led into a vast office; you could have played hurling in it. Benson came round from a massive desk, dressed in a white shirt, the sleeves rolled up.

Just a working stiff.

The pants were part of an Armani suit, and he had Italian brogues, I knew them from my watching of *The Sopranos*. He was tall, built like a weight lifter, tanned features, and eyes that were predatory. He extended a hand, said,

"Benson."

There it was again.

The one name.

I said,

"Taylor."

He made a mock step back, went,

"Whoa, the private dick, to what do I owe the honour?"

There was a tone of barely concealed sarcasm.

"The church has some concerns about you."

He laughed.

"The church, then I really am intrigued."

I said,

"No doubt you've heard of Edge?"

He scoffed.

"Urban myth."

I let that hover, then,

"There is a list of five names and already some of them are deceased."

He levelled his eyes on me, the full brunt of his personality to bear.

"How unfortunate, but—without being callous—why should I care?"

I took a deep breath, said,

"It has been alleged you might have something to do with it."

He was silent, then he chuckled.

"Seriously?"

I nodded.

He weighed all this then asked in a quiet voice,

"What's your interest in these matters?"

"The church hired me to investigate."

He laughed out loud.

"And you come here, expecting what, a confession, ah, that is hilarious."

When his laughter faded, I said,

"Edge have/had the balance of power in this city, remove them and you're the guy."

He shook his head.

"I'm the guy, if you investigated, already you'd know—"

Pause.

"—there is nothing, fucking nothing, in this town that I don't have a say in."

He went to his desk, called security.

Two guys in black uniforms arrived and Benson said,

"Don't come back, and a word of caution, don't nose around in my business."

As they led me away, I asked,

"Apart from the security bit, did you think the meeting went well?"

He was not amused.

"If the church relied on you for any of this, they are in a worse state than I thought."

The security guys had a hold of me on each side, literally flung me onto the street as passersby stopped to witness the spectacle. One guy shouted,

"Taylor, getting thrown out of yet another building, did you think it was the pub?"

I knew that white suit was a mistake.

"In Galway
They believe that,
As they are on the edge of Europe,
They have an edge on the rest of the country.
That edge translates
As a sly friendliness, mostly unmeant."

12

There is a pub in the new Docklands, close to Sheridan's, down a tiny alley, that you must be a real Galwegian to know about. It's called CH's, meaning Clearing House.

For those who are barred from most establishments, it is a refuge. In appearance it looks like a cross between a shebeen and a ruined cottage.

There is a bouncer, a guy named Basil, so called because he binge-watches *Fawlty Towers* and can quote whole episodes.

I was a semiregular.

They had a roaring fire going, a turf fire despite the government intending the banning of turf. It was nearly as heretical as the new Guinness with zero alcohol.

Why?

Huddled near the fire was a former priest who, it was said, had been an exorcist. He had, if you'll forgive the outrageous pun, burned out.

In the past, I had discussions with him about evil. On one occasion, after an hour of my probing questions he uttered,

"Evil is legion."

Another time, I got,

"Evil will come to you if you pursue it."

Now I approached him with hot toddies, his name was Ciaran. He was probably about fifty, but looked eighty, dressed in black, but no white collar. His face was deep lined, but the eyes were alert, a granite grey. I greeted,

"Ciaran, a drink?"

He said,

"Always."

He indicated I should take a seat. I did and raised my glass, to my surprise he clinked glasses.

"Beannacht leat." (*Bless you.*)

I wished him the same and he said,

"I am beyond blessings."

Downer.

He was privy to all kinds of information mainly as he spoke so little, a fervent listener. I asked,

"Are you familiar with Edge?"

He didn't answer for a time, and I wasn't entirely sure he'd heard me, then,

"Stay away from them, they are darkness in action."

I pushed.

"And a man named Benson?"

He looked to the bar, did a finger motion, the barman nodded. Ciaran had privileges denied to most.

Ciaran said,

"Benson is demonic."

I was about to ask more when he added,

"Edge is a group of people who claim to step in and right injustice, but they use that as a cover for all kinds of malignancy and to enrich themselves. Benson wanted to be part of their crew, but they rejected him. So he vowed to erase them, I'm sure some of them have already met violent ends."

"I met with him."

Ciaran shook his head.

"That's not good."

I mused on that a bit but in my chequered career, meeting with dangerous men, and women too, came with the territory.

I said,

"I'll be ready for him."

Ciaran moved back to let the barman place fresh drinks before us, I reached for my wallet, but Ciaran waved that away.

"I have a tab."

Impressive.

An exorcist with a running tab, only in Galway. I said,

"Russell Crowe is making a movie in which he plays an exorcist, what do you think of that?"

He thought about it.

"He has a lived-in face that suits."

We clinked glasses again and he asked,

"Who is your contact with Edge, who approached you?"

I said,

"A woman named Rachel."

Ciaran stared at me with a searching gaze.

"You have feelings for her."

Why deny it?

I nodded and he said,

"There's your Achilles right there."

I protested,

"She's just a conduit."

He gave a bitter smile.

"They don't do conduits, it's all in with them, you are of them or not."

Deep.

I asked,

"Are you still a priest?"

He considered that,

"Are you still a guard?"

In my heart, yes.

He reached in his jacket, produced a small crucifix, handed it to me. It was a gold Celtic one, with a tiny green stone in the middle, the light from the front window caught it in a beam; it cast an almost warm glow.

I said,

"I can't take that."

He gave that small smile again, said,

"Jack Taylor, you need all the protection you can get, both corporeal and metaphysical."

Argue that.

"The true ferocity
Of being
On the edge of sanity
Is the question, do I go?
Back?
Or fuck it all.
Go forth"

13

Martin de Breen was a best-selling author of true crime books.

He ran writing tutorials and advanced writing classes.

These, with his sales and personal appearances, made him a rich man, and as an author of close standing with the literati, he was a vital part of Edge.

He was now dead.

Found in his garage, a pipe attached to his Audi exhaust, it seemed he died of carbon monoxide. The large bumps on his head said otherwise.

The Edge list was diminishing fast.

I met with Rachel, see if we could salvage anything of our tattered relationship.

She told me of the death of Martin de Breen. I had already heard from Owen Daglish, my scarce friend in the Guards, but I let her pour out her grief.

She ended by saying,

"I never thought he would be the type to commit suicide."

There's a type?

I said,

"It wasn't suicide."

She looked like I'd slapped her, which in a way I had.

"I don't believe that."

I said,

"The list of Edge is getting shorter."

She was caught between anger and grief.

"You're trying to scare me."

I said,

"Somebody is."

I asked,

"What do you know about Benson?"

I'd swear she gave a tiny shudder then.

"He wanted to be part of Edge and they turned him down as he's a bully and too reckless."

I pushed.

"You think he might be removing the members of Edge, one by one?"

She was horrified, said,

"Oh, that is insane."

I said,

"I met with him, and he certainly isn't troubled by conscience, plus he despises Edge."

She had no answer to this. I went on a different tack, a perilous one in its own right, as I was fearful of the answer. I asked,

"What about us?"

She didn't reply for an age.

"Oh Jack, I like you and you're never boring but as to a relationship, I'd need to think about it."

A fuck of an answer.

I was home, talking to the dog, who seemed fonder of me.

At least I had someone in my corner. The doorbell rang and I opened it to Father Richard. If possible, he seemed to have grown bigger, or maybe I was shrinking. He came in and the dog made a huge fuss of him.

Fickle beast.

Richard plonkered himself in the sofa, the dog on his lap, said,

"I heard you talking to somebody?"

I said,

"The dog."

This seemed to amuse him greatly.

He said,

"You're, as Kris Kristofferson said, 'a walking contradiction.' "

This was not news to me, and God knows, I'd been called worse by worse.

I made coffee and he asked if I added the Jay.

I had.

He asked,

"No biscuits?"

"No."

He drank the coffee with relish, then,

"Report!"

I loved that. Even in my days as a guard, that word report set my teeth on edge.

"Here's what I've been doing, it's not a report, I don't do reports."

I ran through the meeting with Philomena Dunphy, Benson, and the efforts I'd made to contact the remainder of the list.

Richard glared at me, asked,

"That's it?"

I felt a flash of anger, said,

"Unless I kill Benson, what else can I do?"

He said,

"We're employing you to find solutions, you have done very little as far as I can see."

He struggled to his feet, asked,

"Are you free this evening?"

Was I?

I said,

"Sure."

He gave a wide smile, hints of evil at the edge, said,

"I'm going to treat you to a first-class meal, the best restaurant in town, and see if I can give you some pointers on how to proceed."

I said,

"No."

He was astonished, asked,

"Why?"

I let him simmer.

"I'll be glad to go for a meal, but I will only go to the Galleon in Salthill."

"I don't know it."

I said,

"It's one of the oldest restaurants in the city, the owner Ger is a treasure."

As he was leaving, he said,

"I'll pick you up at eight, dress well."

"You have a car?"

"And a driver."

I was surprised and he added,

"Lighten up, these are the jokes, but I do have a car."

I dressed in my charity shop suit, not the white one, off-white shirt, rowing club tie, and the Doc Martens. I looked like a battered mannequin.

Promptly, a car beeped outside, and I went down to see Richard behind the wheel of a Merc, shining new. I got in the back as Richard left little room with his bulk. I said,

"Now, I have a driver."

He pulled away and he drove like a maniac. I cautioned,

"God almighty, slow down."

He waved a hand.

"Relax, I'm a superb driver."

He found a space beside the Salthill Church and parked effortlessly.

Inside, Ger gave me a warm hug, she looked to Richard who said,

"I can do a hug."

She did.

She didn't comment on his girth but did provide us with a family table.

Discretion.

A waitress came, greeted us effusively, and gave us menus. Richard ordered a ton of food and I said,

"Whoa, I'll never eat all that."

He snarled.

"That's for me, you order your own."

I said to the waitress,

"He's eating for two; one of them is Orson Welles."

Richard fumed,

"You have a very nasty side."

True.

I ordered a steak and a pint.

Richard said,

"A glass of the house wine is fine."

The food came, covered the table.

"You must have skipped lunch."

He looked amazed, answered,

"I never miss meals."

I nearly said,

"It shows."

He dug into a plate of garlic mushrooms, with garlic bread, offered me a taste.

"I might be kissing later so better not."

He sat back.

"Always with the smart mouth."

His main course—main courses—arrived and he dug in.

"Don't feel you have to wait."

He held a spare rib like a pointer, said,

"You can't faze me; I learnt my trade in the Vatican."

My steak arrived and a fresh pint of Guinness, joy to the world.

I asked,

"So how did you become so big?"

I paused then.

"Sorry about big, I meant major player in such shark-infested water?"

He had finished one of his main courses, was now on the second, and seemed to relish every bite. He wiped his mouth, said,

"I was a lowly curate in the Italian countryside and a chance encounter with a cardinal led me to being transferred to the Vatican. I learnt fast that doing favours for the elite was the fast track to high office."

I considered this and he added,

"Primarily, I play dirty."

My steak was good, and I focused on that as he said,

"I like you, Jack; you amuse me, but we both know you're basically a dipso."

Who needed this shite, I stood up.

"Something for you to remember, I play dirty my own self."

He didn't stop eating, said,

"You're a small-time private dick with notions way beyond your abilities; now sit down, I have instructions to issue."

I turned to leave, thanked Ger for her hospitality. She was concerned, asked,

"Was everything all right?"

I assured her it was great, and that the clergy would be paying the tab, she was surprised.

"He's a priest?"

His clerical collar was covered by his thick neck, so she couldn't have known. I said,

"Mainly he's an arsehole, be sure he leaves a decent gratuity."

"As he's a priest, maybe I shouldn't charge him?"

"If it was up to me, I'd charge them all."

Outside, the wind was blowing, sleet and icy rain. I looked in the restaurant window and could see Richard holding out his empty glass.

Not missing me then.

Edge of the world.

President Zelensky arrived in the US and addressed Congress.

A twenty-three-year-old Irish soldier, serving in Lebanon as part of the UN peacekeeping force, was shot dead days before he was due to arrive home.

The East Coast of the US was blitzed by the worst snowstorm of the century.

The World Cup was won by Argentina in what was described by pundits as the best match ever.

14

The days running up to Christmas, I focused on Benson, trying to find some evidence he was involved in the killings of Edge members.

I spoke to former employees, businesspeople, locals, who yielded nothing. The consensus was he was

Tough,

Ruthless,

Brilliant.

But no proof of criminality.

Unless you term hedge funds as the very essence of that.

I was frustrated and at a loss.

But new cases were coming down the line and I welcomed the distraction.

A woman approached me in Garavan's as I was sipping my pint, asked if she might have a moment.

I led her to one of the snugs, noticing she had bad bruising along her left chin, leading down to her neck.

Uh-oh.

Domestics.

Nothing good ever came from them. She was in her early thirties, dressed in an expensive coat and pretty in a down-home fashion.

She said,

"I'm Lucy Fahy and I need your help."

I said,

"Your partner is beating you."

She was taken aback, recovered, said,

"Oh, the bruises, I thought I'd concealed them."

I lied,

"They are not so obvious; it's just I've seen a lot of battered women."

She gasped, went,

"I'm not a battered woman."

"Then why are you here?"

She hung her head.

"My husband beats me."

That sentence still sends a chill dancing along my spine.

I asked,

"Is he a drinker?"

Tears formed in her eyes.

"He used to drink just at weekends but now it's every day and when the drink has a hold, a demon emerges."

The demon drink indeed.

I asked,

"Why don't you go to the Guards?"

A beat.

Then,

"He is a guard."

A guard, and then it came to me,

"Is he Tom Fahy?"

She nodded, asked,

"You know him?"

I said,

"I know his rep."

A bruiser.

He had played hurling for the county and was a feared and lethal player. He didn't go to play; he went to war. He applied the same mindset to his policing. I could only imagine me approaching, asking,

"Why are you beating your wife?"

I said to Lucy,

"You need someone else to deal with him."

She was having none of it, tried,

"But I'll pay you well."

As if.

I said,

"He's out of my league."

In every sense.

She changed tack, said,

"But you used to be a guard."

She began to cry.

Oh fuck.

I can't abide that, and if I'm being played, then played I was.

I said,

"I'll talk to him."

She gripped my hand, tears on her cheeks, said,

"Oh, God bless you."

I'd need more than a blessing, a hurly would be the prayer I invoked.

I rang my one remaining buddy on the force, Owen Daglish, invited him for a pint. He said,

"You'll want something."

I did mock-offended noise.

"Can't I buy a mate a drink without strings?"

He gave a nasty laugh, said,

"With you, Jack, there are always strings, always."

True.

But I did try to be offended.

Didn't work.

My
    Darkest
        Prayer
            —S. A. Cosby

15

I met Owen in the Quays, not my choice as ever since Brad Pitt had a pint there it was swamped by tourists. Owen was sitting by the window, two fresh pints before him.

"One of those for me?"

He looked at his watch, a knockoff Patek Philippe, said,

"Another minute and both would be history."

I took a stool, joined him, he raised his glass.

"Here's to no favours."

I made a sort of affirmative sound, sufficiently vague. The pints went quick as they were perfectly poured, and I signalled for another round. I circled my question for the duration of the second drink and Owen broke first.

"What do you want?"

"Am I paying the bar tab?"

He capitulated, near shouted,

"Just ask me, for Chrissakes."

I asked.

"Tom Fahy?"

He snorted into his glass.

"You don't want to go there."

I stepped away, got some shots of Jay from the counter, brought them back. Owen gave me a long look.

"You do know he's a guard?"

I nodded and he continued.

"Not a guard you want to fuck with."

I said,

"I remember him when he played hurling."

Owen smiled.

"He's still playing except with people's heads."

"Oh."

"Why are you interested in him, except for insanity?"

I said,

"His wife hired me."

Owen groaned.

"No, no, this is not a case you want, tell the woman you can't help her."

I said,

"He's beating her, badly."

Owen knocked back the Jay, did a mock shiver, said,

"He'll massacre you."

How do you find a guard who hurls?

At a hurling match.

Why they pay me the big bucks.

The Galway under-twenty-one team were playing against Athenry on the pitch by the swamp. I huddled up in my Garda coat, wore a tweed flat cap that Rachel had given me, put on my Docs, and headed out.

I looked like I was going to shoot pheasant.

It was raining of course, always at a match, but a sizable crowd had turned out. How to find Tom Fahy?

I knew from Owen he was big, and I heard him before I laid eyes on him. He was shouting abuse at the referee.

I approached slowly, came up behind him, asked,

"Tom Fahy?"

Christ, he was big, towered over me, his face was a riot of burst capillaries and the eyes of a mean ferret. He was wearing an overcoat and a baseball cap that had the Yankees logo on it.

Mixed messages perhaps.

Nothing mixed though about the waves of hostility coming off him.

He snarled,

"Who the fuck are you?"

I decided to grab the bull by the horns, which is always a major misstep. I said,

"I'd like to talk to you about your wife."

And

He punched me full in the face.

My nose was broken.

Yet again.

The previous time had been by a group of vigilantes who were no longer with us.

Thank Christ.

I can't say that having former experience of a broken nose eased the pain somewhat. I fell hard and felt my head crash against the ground. I thought,

"At least I'm not unconscious."

Did this help?

It didn't.

I got to my feet, felt faint.

I staggered back into the crowd, blood pouring down my face and though half-blind from pain and shock, I found a bench and sat, put my head back to stop the bleeding, thought,

"It didn't bleed the last time."

This was of scant comfort. My vision was blurred, and a tremor shot through my body. A man approached, asked,

"Might I take your picture?"

Really?

Like fucking seriously?

I managed to utter,

"Fuck off."

But he took the picture anyway and I was in no state to prevent him.

The

   Next

      Day

Lucy Fahy died under the wheels of a bus.

16

I was back in hospital, due to a severe concussion from when I hit my head after Fahy had broken my nose.

I was also on the front page of the local paper, the photo of me bleeding from my nose and the headline,

"Thuggery at hurling match."

The tone of the article suggested that I was the instigator of the trouble. So I could add sport hooligan to my résumé.

I called Rachel as soon as I was allowed to sit up in the hospital; she came and I gave her the keys to my apartment to take care of the dog.

She came but didn't bring grapes, she brought wrath. Gave me a rollocking of epic proportions. Her parting shot was,

"You don't deserve a dog."

Low blow, I thought.

The doctor, referring to the time two years ago that I'd been in a coma, stated,

"This is not your first rodeo."

I fumed.

"You use expressions like that with all your patients?"

He gave me the medical smile, a blend of malice, patience, and mild interest.

He said they'd be keeping me for observation.

It was two days before I learned that Lucy Fahy had gone under a bus.

Owen Daglish came to visit but not in his guard uniform. Thank God; with the photo in the paper and then a guard at my bedside, I'd be the focus of undue attention.

He did bring a bottle of Jay, said,

"Better than grapes?"

He also had plastic cups and, looking around carefully, he poured two fine measures, handed me one.

"Sláinte amach."

I agreed, took a gulp, and felt that delicious tremor run through me, not sure what it did to the concussion, but it did hit the reckless button.

He put his cup down, said,

"I have some bad news."

Then told me of the death of Lucy Fahy. I was shocked, asked,

"They think she did it deliberately?"

He shrugged.

"Her husband is a guard so not a lot of interest."

I felt a rush of pure rage, so much that my hands shook. Owen said,

"Whoa, it was probably an accident and you're in hospital so move on."

I simmered.

I held my cup out and he shook his head, said,

"No, you need to rest up, I'll give you the bottle when you get out."

I snarled.

"I think I'd have preferred grapes."

My photo being on the front page of the paper gave me a notoriety I didn't welcome. When you're lying in a hospital bed, low profile is what you need.

My nose was reset, kind of.

The concussion was finally beginning to improve but it brought blinding headaches and who could I call?

No one.

I had hoped to be there for say, a week, tops.

No.

So, I missed Christmas, and I sure missed my dog. I knew Rachel would treat him well, but I worried he would bond with her.

He did.

The treacherous little bastard.

I was finally released after a few weeks, did score some heavy-duty painkillers. Chase those with the Jay and nirvana was a breath away.

Back at my apartment, Rachel had laid in groceries but no booze, a message. No dog and the place felt empty without him.

I called Rachel and she said she'd come by. I pushed my luck, tried, "Grab a six pack, I'll pay you."

She hung up.

In my absence, the pope, Rosenberger as they called him in Galway, who had retired years ago, was now dead, so heavy ceremonies in the Vatican.

Ronaldo was signed by a Saudi team for megamillions and in his next match, he was due to meet Messi, tickets were gold. One punter paid two million for a ticket.

The world had continued in its dance of madness.

Prince Harry's book, Spare, was out and was the best-selling book ever in the publishing world.

I muttered,

"Spare me."

Lisa Marie Presley died two days after the Golden Globe awards. She had seen Elvis, the biopic, get best actor award. Gina Lollobrigida died. She was ninety-five.

At the Lunar New Year celebrations in Los Angeles, a gunman, aged seventy-two, opened fire and killed ten people, injuring scores of others. He then, after a twelve-hour pursuit, turned the gun on himself.

Ireland gets fourteen Oscar nominations.

17

I was walking along Shop Street, wondering if I'd drop into Dubray bookshop when a woman stopped me, she planted herself right in front of me, asked,

"Are you Tommy Taylor's son?"

I was, said,

"I am."

She near spat,

"He was a real waste of space."

Her words rocked me, and the tone was utterly malignant. I took a breath, then reached for my wallet, asked,

"How much did he owe you?"

She was puzzled, knocked from her high horse, said,

"He didn't borrow money from me."

I smiled, said,

"Of course not, he wouldn't be caught dead talking to the likes of you."

Rachel came to visit, without the dog. I asked if the dog pined at all for me.

No.

I told her about Tom Fahy and the death of his wife. I didn't give an opinion of what I thought.

Waited.

She said,

"You think he pushed his wife under a bus?"

"I do."

She gave me the granite look, no warmth lingering.

"You love trouble."

And?

She then added,

"You'll be getting your hurly ready."

Indeed.

She shook her head, then changed tack.

"Edge has disbanded, the remaining members have moved out of the city, so Benson is now the power in the town."

Adding fuel to her sense of outrage, I said,

"I'll deal with him later."

She sighed, said,

"You'll need more than a hurly."

I gave her my best smile.

Said,

"I have motivation."

She left in a huff, throwing,

"You're impossible."

True.

I had lost a lady and a dog, without even trying.

While I considered the slow deconstruction of my life, the phone rang. The Mother Superior of the nun's convent. My last case, a man had been attacking nuns and the Mother Superior had engaged me to help. The case had been solved, not due to me but with the help of Edge.

I had developed a sharp spiky odd friendship with the nun. She'd insisted I call her Therese. I tried.

Growing up, nuns were mysterious creatures who you'd never address by their names. I heard now,

"Mr. Taylor, it's Therese, the Mother Superior, do you remember me?"

Like who could forget?

"I do, how can I help you?"

She answered,

"Would you come and see me?"

I would.

Said,

"I will."

The convent was in Nun's Island, but a short prayer from the cathedral. I had once lived in this area and held no fond memories of that time, much like every other place I'd been.

I walked up the long driveway and was struck by two things.

You could hear the birds singing and yet there was a sense of utter silence. A silence of calm, that things were as you would have wished.

I rang the bell and a young nun opened the door, she looked about sixteen. She gave me a radiant smile, welcomed,

"Mr. Taylor, how nice to see you again."

When nuns remember you, you are either doing something half right or the very opposite. She stepped aside, said,

"You know the way to Mother Superior's office."

I nodded, walked to the door at the end of the corridor, knocked, and heard,

"Come in."

Therese was seated behind a large desk, ablaze with files, she stood up, extended her hand, said,

"I don't think you do hugs?"

Something about her brought out the devil in me, I tried,

"I'm staying away from hugs one day at a time."

She asked if I'd like tea, coffee, water?

My last visit, she'd produced a bottle of Jay but not this time. She indicated I should sit.

"You were a tremendous help to us in our time of dire need."

I told the truth, said,

"I had help."

"The assailant who attacked our nuns is, I believe, in a coma."

I nodded.

She continued,

"When he comes round, do you plan on seeing him?"

"Most definitely."

She didn't like the tone of this, said,

"Forgiveness is a real blessing."

I gave her my wolf smile.

"Not really in my life."

She was upset.

"We'll pray for you and him."

I took a deep breath, said,

"I don't much relish being in the same prayer as that piece of garbage."

She sighed.

"We need your help yet again."

I said I'd try, if I could, she said,

"We recently got a gift of a golden crucifix, inlaid with jewels, a beautiful piece and of tremendous value. We decided to put it on display for a short time so people could see and appreciate it, but last Sunday, someone stole it."

I said nothing and she added,

"We will of course pay you for your time."

"Experience teaches.

First the test

Then the lesson."

—With respect to Oscar Wilde

18

To find the nuns' cross, I went to the best source.

Thieves.

A reflection of my life that I knew so many. I did the rounds of their hangouts and finally hit pay dirt in Kennedy's bar on Eyre Square. A thief I knew by the name of Jordan, no first name, was nursing a pint in a window seat. We were on reasonably good terms due to my getting him a suspended sentence rather than jail time.

I bought him a pint, surveyed him. He was in his late fifties, with long grey hair, a broken nose much like my own, he was lean like a greyhound and just as fast if Guards were in the neighbourhood.

He greeted,

"Jack, good to see you."

Mm.

Among thieves, he was regarded as upper echelon if such there be. Meaning he didn't bother with the nickel-and-dime trade, there were enough junkies infesting that branch of the business. Literally smash-and-grab merchants. Jordan went for the high end of the market.

We killed the first pint with sundry stories of the town. He said,

"Edge is no more."

Which led me to the main topic. But before I could broach it, he said one hundred twenty years ago, one of the Aran islands sold thirteen skulls to Trinity College Dublin and now they want them back. I mulled over that, and he added,

"I offered to steal them back, but they seemed quite horrified at the concept."

I circled my main concern, asked.

"Would a solid gold cross be in your range?"

He signalled for another round, said,

"You're picking up the tab?"

"Of course."

The drinks came, nice creamy heads, seemed almost a shame to disrupt them but we did. He sank half of his in one swallow.

"Where would such a treasure be held?"

The game was afoot, I said,

"A convent."

He was quiet, then,

"Tricky to break into such a place."

I agreed, said,

"Would take an artist of rare ability."

He revealed a dazzling smile, said,

"Indeed."

I asked,

"How much would an artist get for such a treasure?"

He considered.

"Five large."

I pushed,

"Who might buy such an item?"

He gave me a searching look, then,

"The man who took over from Edge."

Benson.

Now to push my luck, I asked,

"And to steal it back?"

He let out a breath.

"Not sure that would be possible. Benson has state-of-the-art security."

Time for the old flattery gig.

"An artist, though, he'd see it as a real triumph."

He laughed, said,

"He might."

Then he went dark, added,

"A few years back, a thief broke into Benson's home, few days later he was found with both his legs smashed to smithereens."

"How much was the cross sold for?"

No hesitation.

"Five grand."

I let that sum whistle in the air then I asked,

"To steal it back again?"

He shook his head, said,

"You're talking ten grand and the added risk of the wrath of Benson."

"My client is a nun, as you'll have guessed, and that amount of cash is way beyond her means."

He gave a bitter chuckle.

"Those nuns sit on property worth millions, poor they ain't. I mean they lose a cross; they have tons of gold stuff in the vaults."

I signalled for two shots of Jay, said,

"It was worth a shot, well two shots anyway."

He eased a bit, said,

"Lemme think about it."

Which meant he was halfway toward doing it.

He said,

"Benson is a real piece of work, over ten years, he had gradually diluted the influence and power of Edge. One by one, he got rid of the members. He was aided by their own interfighting, they were so busy looking out for personal gain that he literally sneaked up on them, one by one."

I asked him,

"What do you know about Tom Fahy?"

He said,

"I need a smoke."

We went outside, joined a huddled group, like the outcasts of society. He offered a cigarette, Rothmans.

"I'm trying to quit."

He gave a quiet laugh, said,

"Next, you'll be off the drink."

Right.

He hadn't forgotten my query, said,

"Fahy is a nasty bollix, steer clear of him, plus he's a guard so kind of untouchable."

Then he asked,

"Why?"

I told him of how Lucy Fahy had come to me for help, her husband was beating her. I added how I approached him, and he broke my nose.

Jordan gave a loud inadvertent laugh, said,

"Man, you are one crazy bastard."

Sky News was on and an earthquake of 7.8 on the Richter scale hit Turkey and Syria. The death toll was twelve thousand and rising.

The church was going to drop *Father* from the Lord's Prayer and replace it with *Love*!

The woke brigade was on its uppers.

Ireland could no longer house the refugees pouring into the country and in freezing cold, many were housed in tents.

The new proposal was that arriving refugees would be given food vouchers and must source their own accommodation.

Zelensky was in London, addressing Parliament and pleading for fighter jets.

Massive fires were burning through Chile.

Jordan looked at me, said,

"The world is full fucked."

I called at the convent; the door answered by the same small nun.

She said,

"We'll convert you yet, Mr. Taylor."

I smiled, asked,

"But converted to what?"

She suppressed a giggle, said,

"You're a devil."

Indeed.

I was shown into the office of the Mother Superior, who was finishing up a call, stood to greet me; for a moment, a hug hovered, but dissipated, thank God.

"Good to see you Mr. Taylor."

She indicated I should take a seat, asked,

"A drink?"

And produced the bottle of Jay, two Galway crystal glasses, poured liberally. She asked,

"Do you require water?"

I shuddered in mock horror.

"'Twould be heresy."

She enjoyed the ecclesiastical banter, raised her glass.

"God bless."

I answered,

"You are too."

I took a sip, trying to show some etiquette; normally, I'd wallop it in one and wait for the warm hit. Therese barely touched hers. I said,

"I have kind of good news, certainly plenty of not so good."

She waited, so I launched,

"I found the cross, and the thief who stole it, he got five thousand euro for it."

She gasped, took a larger sip of the Jay, waited.

I said,

"The thief can steal it back, not easily, but he can do it; the problem is he wants a shitload, whoops sorry, a lot of cash for it."

She was quiet, then,

"How much?"

I took a deep breath.

"Ten grand."

She went,

"Jesus, Mary, and Joseph."

I said,

"There is another way."

Her hands were intertwined, with a slight tremor, she waited.

I said,

"The man who has it is named Benson; you could ask him to return it."

I thought this was a terrible idea but felt I had to at least float it. She levelled her gaze on me.

"I don't think that would be appropriate."

I said the thing I was hoping I wouldn't have to say,

"You want me to ask him."

"You know him?"

"Only by reputation."

She took another tiny sip of the Jay, asked,

"And that is?"

I told the truth, said,

"He's the devil."

She considered this then,

"I don't think I'll be visiting him."

Which left just stealing it.

"Will I steal it so?"

She was horrified though a little bit excited.

"Good heavens, I couldn't condone that."

I stood up, thanked her for the drink, said,

"Don't give up hope."

She laughed.

"I'm a nun, hope is what we do."

"Some people
Regard pity
As a powerful
Tool."

19

"You're to be pitied,"

Said Benson,

To me.

I had bluffed my way past his ice receptionist and stood before his desk.

The gold crucifix was on a shelf behind him. I decided to get right to it and asked,

"I'd like you to return that cross."

He stood up, cut an imposing figure, his jacket off, sleeves rolled up, displaying strong arms, on the verge of turning to fat, a silk tie with a gold tie clip, in, would you believe, the shape of a cross.

Who knew tiepins were still a thing?

That's when he snarled the pity line.

I said,

"A pity would be if it were known you stole from the nuns."

He pressed a button on the desk and two security guys appeared almost immediately. Benson said,

"Throw this loser out."

They did. Again.

My apartment was in Ocean Towers, but a wave from the seafront. I had a bay window where I could sit and watch the tides. It made me yearn but for what I didn't know. There was a knock on my door, I opened it to a woman.

An attractive one.

Auburn hair, pretty face just short of beautiful. She was dressed in a sweatshirt, jeans, and soft brown leather boots. Her age was in that vague forty to fifty range.

She held out her hand, said,

"I'm Keelan, your new neighbour."

I took her hand, said,

"Jack, Jack Taylor."

I invited her in, but she demurred with,

"I can't right now but I'm having a drinks party tomorrow at eight, be lovely if you could come."

I had begun tracking Tom Fahy, my broken nose was motive enough to do so. For a week, he seemed to follow the same pattern.

Go to work.

The pub after.

Then home.

I wasn't entirely sure what I was going to do to him, but hopefully something primeval. I broke into his home while he was at work. No security system; being a guard, he was complacent. The house was your basic two up, two down. It was a mess, dishes in the sink, clothes thrown any which way.

I had learnt how to bypass passwords. A young kid named Jesse was some kind of wunderkind and I had saved him from bullies in the past. He thought I was, wait for it,

"Cool."

I've been a lot of things, most of them shady, but cool?

No.

I sat at Fahy's computer, bypassed his password, then, using a USB stick, I uploaded a pile of data on his hard drive. I noticed a complete lack of any sign of his wife Lucy. No photos, and all her clothes had been removed.

Fahy was a man moving on. Not if I could help it.

I got out of there, bought a burner phone, then phoned the vice squad, laid a story on them, and gave his address.

Two days later, it was on the news that a senior guard had been arrested for child pornography, a thousand images on his hard drive.

You might say I'd thrown him under a bus.

Owen Daglish rang me, said he wanted to buy me a pint.

A rib broke in the devil.

We met in Busker Brownes; they do a mean jazz session on Sunday mornings.

Owen was dressed in a wax Barbour coat, black cords, and looked like a Brit squire who'd wandered beyond the pale. I said,

"You look very country field."

He had the pints ready, I raised my glass, toasted,

"To Ukraine."

He gave me a long look, asked,

"You heard about Tom Fahy? I never had him pegged as a kiddie fiddler."

"That is an ugly description."

He sipped at his pint, said,

"Solved your dilemma what to do about him."

His words were loaded.

I said,

"It would be some whiz to lodge those images on his laptop."

I put up my hands, said,

"As you know I'm a Luddite with technology."

He was quiet, then,

"I vaguely remember you helping out a kid who was some sort of super geek."

I gave a tight smile.

"Justice was done."

A few months back, I'd been walking along the canal, at the lower end that backs on to the Róisín Dubh. The Róisín was where bands with edge got to play. You might not be a success in commercial terms but in terms of street cred, playing the Róisín was the biz.

The canal always brought back childhood memories of fishing for eels. We'd bring them home and my dad would fry them on the Aga, a big old stove that was over fifty years old and still good to go.

Thing is, I never liked eels.

There was a man who lived at the end of our street, he told my father,

"I had an eel on the pan and decided a slice of bacon would be good, but the eel ate it!"

Before I turned into the canal, I'd been in the handball alley in the college. I sometimes went there, with my hurly and a stack of tennis balls; then for a good hour, I whacked the bejaysus out of the balls. Best therapy I know, just wallop the hell out of my system.

As I walked along the canal, I saw three young men, they had a man on the ground and were taking turns kicking him. I shouted,

"Hey, shitheads."

They turned as one. I moved fast, left my holdall down, picked up the first one and threw him in the canal, then I reached for my hurly and took out the legs of the second.

The third ran.

I helped the man from the ground, that's how I met Jesse, the hacker.

He was twenty-one but looked about fourteen, with a mop of black curly hair. He had one of those faces that seemed always ready to smile.

He wasn't smiling now, he looked at me with amazement, went,

"Wow."

He was unsteady on his feet, and I advised him to take some deep breaths, he did and after a few minutes, he said,

"Thank you."

I asked,

"Why were they kicking you?"

"Prime."

Prime? Like Amazon Prime?

He produced a can from his battered jacket. It was red and black with *Prime* in bold letters. I asked,

"They were attacking you for a soda?"

He laughed, revealing braces on his teeth; he said,

"Prime is the brainchild of a YouTuber and a podcaster; they created a drink for young people, adults are excluded. It's a thing for now."

I asked,

"And is it booze or loaded with dope or what?"

He popped the can, said,

"Take a swig, you sure deserve it."

I did.

It tasted of a whole lot of sugar, fizzy water, and a hell of a caffeine load, traces of coconut too. I handed it back to him, said,

"I don't get it."

He smiled again, said,

"That's the point, you're not the demographic."

That's how I hooked up with Jesse.

He came from a broken home; alcoholism didn't run in his family. It galloped.

In his early teens, he'd been thrown out of his home, such as it was, and learned early how to survive. It was a point of pride with him that he'd never once slept rough.

Sure, he slept rough but managed always to be indoors; said to me,

"A kid like me, they'd have eaten me alive."

He discovered that he had a unique gift for all things technical. Such geeks were the new rock stars. He freelanced for the big companies and was always in demand. I asked him,

"Why are you always smiling?"

The smile again, he said,

"They find it hard to beat you when you have a smile on your face. My father used to say, 'I'll knock that fucking smile off yah.' He didn't."

Google, Microsoft, PayPal, Twitter, Dell had all announced redundancies and cuts in their staff. Those such as Jesse, their special talents would never be dispensed with.

As the month of February ended, I asked him how he would disable a company like Benson had. He made the sound,

"Whoosh."

Not good.

Then the smile again, he said,

"Difficult but possible."

He went on to talk about

Firewalls,

Trojan horses,

Thor,

Dark net,

And my eyes began to glaze over.

He asked if I wanted some Prime to shake me up, I said,

"I'm good, thanks."

He was a good kid, I liked him a lot. He asked if I played frisbee.

I gave him the look, asked,

"Take a wild guess?"

A while later, while I was considering how to persuade Jordan to steal back the cross, I got a call from Jesse. He was in the process of buying a penthouse in Nun's Island and the company, wary of his youth, needed an adult reference.

I did that for him, and he said,

"All these mentions of nuns, I came across a debut novel you might like."

Oh.

I don't much get gifts and if I do, I try not to look them in the mouth, so I said,

"Thank you."

The book was

Scorched Grace

by
Margot Douaihy.
It featured a nun named Sister Holiday who,
Wait for this,
Was
A chain-smoking,
Tattooed,
Lesbian,
Biker.
Phew-oh.
Imagine if I gave it to Mother Therese!

20

The party.

I got a crisp white shirt from the charity shop, plus a jazzy sports jacket and black cord jeans. I bought a twenty-two-year-old bottle of Jay.

Good to go.

I hadn't shaved and was trying for the three-day Jason Statham gig. The sports jacket made me look like an arsehole. I had the gold Down Syndrome pin, topped off with a Galway United tie. Tied loose as if I was *Devil may care.*

The overall image was of a disbarred accountant.

Time?

What is the smart hour to arrive? You don't want to seem too keen, nor do you want to roll in half pissed at midnight. I settled for 10:45.

I had been to the market outside St. Nicholas's Church. Bought a handwoven St. Brigid's cross. Years ago, a mate was moving into his new home, and I gave him one of those crosses to keep the house safe.

The very next day, the house was burgled, and the thieves took everything except for the cross.

I was anxious, the only parties I'd attended were simply piss-ups. Mostly I remember little of them.

I checked myself in the mirror and saw a battered wild man in a god-awful jacket. I took a deep breath, muttered,

"Let's party."

And headed next door.

The door to my neighbour's was answered by Keelan, who was

Wearing a tracksuit. There seemed to be about twenty people present and all were in casual gear. I looked like I'd come to read the meter.

I handed Keelan the Jay and the St. Brigid's cross and she went,

"Oh!"

The fuck?

She asked,

"Did I not mention it was a frozen margarita evening?"

No.

Trust a battered alky to bring whiskey to a tequila fest.

Keelan handed me a drink, said,

"Welcome to my new home."

I don't do mingling. As in approach a group of people and introduce myself.

I gulped the drink rapidly and wow, what an instant wallop. Who the fuck needed Jay, I could sink these babies for the evening and another one or two, I might mingle.

A group of people were gathered round a central figure, who was regaling them with some apparently hilarious tale. Keelan urged me,

"Come meet our guest of honour."

Not me then.

That was the tequila whispering malice.

I let her lead me over to

Benson.

Keelan said with great enthusiasm,

"George, may I present Jack Taylor."

The group fell silent as Benson barked,

"Taylor! The private dick, I had him thrown out of my office. Twice."

Silence reigned.

I broke it with,

"'Tis true, but they were very courteous security, they only called me a bollix once."

I turned to Keelan, said,

"I have to go; I can't be in the same room as a psycho."

And

I left.

The tequila was coursing in my veins, so I decided to walk along the prom, listen to the waves. It calms me so.

There was a nip in the breeze, and I was ill dressed in the sports jacket. A homeless guy beseeched me,

"I'll take anything."

So I gave him the jacket and twenty euro.

The evening wasn't a complete wash.

"Linger"
Dolores O'Riordan
The Cranberries

21

I met Jordan, the ace burglar, in Richardson's pub at the top of Eyre Square.

On the wall is a plaque to the poet Rita Higgins.

Jordan was standing at the bar with another man, a man dressed to kill. Sharp suit, sharper haircut, and that vibe of

Don't fuck with me.

I approached and the man nodded at Jordan and left. Jordan shook my hand, said of the departed man,

"Another satisfied customer."

I didn't ask.

He wouldn't have told me anyway. One of the reasons he stayed out of jail was his ability to be discreet. He ordered the pints and Sean, the bar guy, said,

"Take a seat, gents. I'll bring 'em over."

We sat by the window, could see a tight group of refugees huddled under the trees on the square. We were now officially out of accommodation for those arriving at Dublin Airport. Seventy thousand from Ukraine had already arrived.

Jordan said,

"You're looking well, by that I mean you're full of devilment."

He was right, the devil was loud and roaring in my soul.

Blame a tequila hangover.

I said,

"We're on."

Jordan was surprised, went,

"You mean steal the cross again?"

"Yup."

He shook his head,

"Benson will have top-of-the-line technical security."

I smiled, said,

"I have a young man who can cripple all that for one hour, nine to ten, this Thursday; can you manage in that time frame?"

He mulled it over,

"That could work."

I handed over an envelope, said,

"It's not what you asked, but treat it as a down payment."

He gave me a long look, asked,

"Are you prepared for the fallout? You rob a psycho like Benson, shit is going to rain down."

I said,

"I want him off-balance so I can seriously fuck him over."

He gave a low whistle,

"You're a piece of work, Jack, who'd believe you'd be the hit man for nuns."

Maybe it would earn me some brownie points in heaven. God knows, I needed all the good karma I could get.

"If you weren't
Twitchy,
Driving in a hostile country
With no lifeline,
You were probably
A sociopath."

—David McCloskey
Damascus Station

22

I had Jesse primed to knobble Benson's IT programs and Jordan was set to go.

I'd be well pleased if I could get the cross back to the nuns. I was in no doubt that Benson would strongly suspect my involvement. I wasn't worried at the prospect, but I should have been.

I was remembering more and more incidents from my childhood. Friday was always a tense day as the rent man was due. He carried a thick ledger and your payment, or usually nonpayment, was inscribed. Amby Roche was his name and we always addressed him as Mister. His son was now one of the finest engineers in the city.

Once a month, a woman would come to our home, she was from the council and had her own key. She didn't knock, just barged in and inspected the house, God forbid you'd changed anything from the meagre set up. I hated that bitch.

Amby Roach was the only rent man liked by the neighbours. He had compassion. Then after the rent man had been, the priest would call, and I remember him beseeching my mother.

"Surely you have a spare half a crown somewhere?"

She didn't.

We didn't.

I was counting how many weeks it had been since I smoked a cigarette.

On the table was a steaming mug of black coffee. Outside my window were two robins and a goldfinch. There was a rich peace in watching them.

My doorbell rang and I admitted Keelan, my new neighbour. She was dressed in a navy tracksuit, her hair pulled back in a severe ponytail. She looked fresh and appealing.

She said,

"I am so sorry about the debacle of the party."

I shrugged it off, offered coffee.

"Have you decaf?"

Like seriously?

I said,

"Sure."

Went to the kitchen, poured her a cup of real caffeine, brought it out. She wrapped her hands round the mug as if she were cold. Took a sip, said,

"Tastes like the real thing."

I gave her my best smile, said,

"It's all in the blend."

She was circling round something.

"There's bad blood between you and Mr. Benson?"

I said,

"He stole a cross from some nuns."

She wasn't sure where to go from there, went with echo.

"Cross?"

I said,

"He stole the cross from the nuns. I confronted him and, as he said, he had me slung out of the office."

She looked down at the floor, seemed troubled, then,

"This is awkward."

I waited; I can do awkward.

She said,

"I'm involved with George."

Fuck.

I have a bad drop in me, a nastiness that I try to rein in.

But doesn't always rein too good.

I asked,

"Is he married?"

Her face darkened, she near spat,

"How dare you!"

So, I guess, yes.

I said,

"I'm thinking our budding friendship took a dive."

She headed for the door.

"George said you were a pitiful souse."

I gave her a radiant smile, asked,

"What's a souse?"

"She was a nice Protestant girl from Indiana. She'd steal, but she stole for the thrill of it. . . . A good thief doesn't steal for the thrill.

He steals for the money.

And

The best thief of all steals

Because

He's a thief."

—Lawrence Block

Out

On

The

Cutting

Edge

23

Jordan called me, said,

"Job done."

Succinct.

We arranged for him to come to my apartment. He showed up, carrying a heavy backpack. Laid it down on the floor, said,

"That geek kid of yours, he did as he planned, knocked out all Benson's security for an hour. I took a few other items to show the cross was not the main object." He upturned the pack, spilled items on the floor.

Montblanc pens.

Mobile phones.

A bronze statuette of Michael Collins.

A wad of twenty-euro notes.

And

The cross.

It glowed amid the items.

I said,

"The nuns will pray for you."

I got the bottle of Jay, poured us healthy ones,

"Here's to you, boyo."

Jordan said,

"It's been a time since I did a job and I got to tell you, it was a fucking rush, man, when the adrenaline kicked in, I could have stolen for Ireland."

He finished the drink, and I poured him another, he indicated the loot, asked,

"Anything you want?"

"No, the cross is sufficient."

He said,

"I'll have to lie low for a time. Benson will go berserk, and I'm bound to be on the list of suspects."

He grabbed the backpack, gave a huge smile.

"It's been fun; anytime you want a robbery, give me a shout."

I figured the loot he had went some ways to pay him and told him I'd manage the remainder soon.

He shrugged it off.

"When I fence this lot, I'll be well paid."

When he was gone, I placed the cross on the coffee table, the early sun caught its silhouette and threw off a golden light. The Mother Superior would be delighted.

I rang the convent, got Therese and announced,

"The cross has been found."

She gave a small whoopee, said,

"Ah, you blessed man."

I have been called many things, few complimentary, but blessed was a first.

I'd take it.

St. Patrick's Day arrived, and the country went on the piss. It was an opportunity to be legless and not be condemned. I skipped the parade, something about them makes me want to howl.

An international criminal warrant has been issued on Putin. His response was to drive himself to Crimea, and he was due to meet with the Chinese leader. The Chinese continued to support him.

Trump was due to be indicted for payment to the woman named Stormy for services rendered, he was already urging his followers to

Protest.

Protest.

Protest.

Shades of the January storming on the US Capitol already looming.

The world burned more every day. The North Korean Kim was test-firing nuclear missiles on a nigh weekly basis.

You had to ask,

How can we survive?

"When we finally find what
We have been looking for in the darkness,
We nearly always discover
That it was exactly that.
Darkness."

—Håkan Nesser
Mind's Eye

24

Jordan
Was thrown
From the roof
Of the Hardiman hotel,
His right hand
Had been severed,
As is the custom in the Middle East?
For thieves.

I was shattered at the news about Jordan. Owen Daglish had come to my apartment and shared the grisly details. He said,

"I know you were mates with the guy."

Mates.

I said,

"I've known him a long time, even before he decided on a criminal career."

Owen sighed, asked,

"Don't you have, like, any regular friends, I mean ordinary folk? Does everyone in your battered universe have a story?"

I said,

"There's a neon sign above my head that welcomes the weird and marginalised."

Owen had brought a bottle of the Jay, poured us both a sinful measure, took a sip, grimaced, said,

"Here's the thing, there is a rumour that Benson, your own bête noire, was burglarised. It was hushed up as Benson doesn't advertise being vulnerable, some serious items were supposedly taken, and to rob Benson, you'd need to be damn lucky, reckless, or a highly skilled burglar. Not many of these about. But your buddy, Jordan, Lord rest him, was for sure in the top tier of thieves."

He stared at me, I asked,

"Is there a question in there?"

He produced a vape, sucked on it, said,

"I'm wondering if Jordan might not have shared his accomplishment with you?"

I was fixated on the vape, it produced a literal cloud of vapour.

"Top thieves stay top by not sharing."

Owen looked at the vape, said,

"I'd kill for a real cig."

Then he said,

"If Benson thinks you had any part, any input at all, you'll be sailing off a roof."

Owen took a fine wallop of the Jay, added,

"Seeing as we're speculating, shooting the shit, I heard vague rumours of a valuable cross. Said item that Benson is very keen to reacquire."

I nearly laughed.

"A cross he stole from nuns."

Owen threw his hands up in despair, spilling Jay on his suit, muttered,

"That's exactly what I'm getting at. You know stuff and it is always of the lethal kind."

He stood up, brushed at his suit, said,

"Jack, seriously, don't fuck with guy. Not only does he have people flung from rooftops, but took the time to chop off the poor bastard's hand."

He got the door, paused, asked,

"You are working for the nuns again?"

I said,

"In an advisory role."

He clamped a beefy arm on my shoulder, said,

"Don't."

I met with Jesse on a bench at Spanish Arch. Mid-March and already the area was kicking with tourists.

Jesse was gone full goth for the meet, kohl eyes, pure white face, the makeup congealing at the collar, black jeans and black Docs and what appeared to be a black cape. I asked,

"Are you a roadie for The Cure or a misguided Marilyn Manson stooge or, at a stretch, a confused Batman?"

He said, offering a bare arm, a new tattoo with the letter *J* intwined with snakes. He said,

"The *J* is for—"

I hushed him, said,

"Not a name to be throwing around; the animals who threw our friend off the roof are on the hunt."

25

Jordan's funeral.

Most funerals I attend are wet, windy, god-awful affairs. This day, a Monday, the sun was splitting the rocks.

And

A large crowd.

The undertaker was Clare Ann Irwin, a stunning looker who was the Galway Rose, in every sense. She had, with her father Joe, revolutionised the funeral craft in the city.

As we stood over the grave, she gave me a shy smile. It amused her greatly that I had them on speed dial. That says most of what my life is, undertakers on my fast track.

Mo léan géar. (*Woe is me.*)

A very striking woman was standing near her, dressed in black, she seemed to be grief-shattered.

The priest droned,

"Life is full of misery."

No joy there.

The large crowd consisted of

Thieves,

The homeless,

Some very well-dressed men in suits (these would be your upper echelon of thieves),

Vagrants,

Two guards.

After, Clare Ann announced that refreshments would be provided in Toner's. She brought the grieving woman to me, said,

"Jack, this is Jordan's sister."

She had what can best be described as a cute face, now streaked with tears and mascara. I offered her my hanky, she gave a small smile, asked,

"Do people even use those anymore?"

I managed,

"Old school."

The pub was but a drink from the cemetery, and that's a cautionary tale of itself.

The sister's name was Shiv, short for Siobhan, like the character in *Succession*. She linked my arm, asked,

"Will you walk me down?"

I would and did.

She smelled of patchouli, a scent I'd always loved since hippy times.

When she linked me, I felt a jolt of pure adrenaline, Jesus, who gets frisky at a burial? I remembered the story about Ryan O'Neal hitting on his daughter at the funeral of her mother. In fairness, and let's face it, there is fuck-all fairness nowadays, Ryan didn't realise it was his own daughter, Tatum.

As we walked, me in a dizzy void, she said,

"You're Jack Taylor."

Indeed.

I nodded, she continued,

"You were his best friend."

What the fuck?

I was the bollix who got him killed.

I did not share this.

She said,

"That one time, he was in Mountjoy Prison, you visited him regularly."

He was only ever nicked the one time and got two years. After that, he swore to always work solo. He'd been part of a gang who targeted the homes of the rich.

The pub was jammed, a free bar brings the masses. There was a full catering service, but Shiv declined, settled for a vodka tonic. I had a coffee. I wanted a blast of Jay but felt some decorum was in order.

We got a seat near the window, Shiv studied me, I felt myself wilt under the scrutiny. Finally, she asked,

"What happened to my brother?"

I said,

"He robbed the wrong people."

Tears filled her eyes again, she faltered,

"But his hand, why that horror?"

I said,

"Savages."

People kept approaching, offering condolences and she said,

"Jordan seems to have been well liked."

I told the truth,

"He was loved."

She thought about that, then,

"I'm glad you were his friend."

Phew-oh.

Then a man in a fine suit came over, said,

"Jordy was the best thief in the city."

She mumbled,

"Thank you."

And rolled her eyes at me.

We stayed for about an hour, then she gathered her things.

"I'm going to my hotel, I feel exhausted."

I offered to walk her, and she smiled, said,

"No need, and you can now have a drink."

Busted.

We had exchanged phone numbers. I didn't really think I'd hear from her. I was tempted to call her and ask if she'd like a drink, dinner, anything.

But I didn't.

The guilt over Jordan's death hung over me.

Two days later, I was sipping at my morning coffee when the phone buzzed.

Shiv.

In a terrible state. Weeping and nigh hysterical.

I kept my voice low,

"What's happened?"

I could hear her taking deep breaths, then,

"A hand has been left on Jordan's grave."

Fuck.

I asked,

"Where are you?"

"At the grave, the Guards are here, and a forensic team have taken the—"

She paused, grabbing for calm.

"—the hand, I mean Jordan's hand, I think it's his, there was a claddagh ring on his finger."

I said,

"Stay there, I'll be right up."

I threw on my Garda all-weather coat, black 501s, my Docs, moving fast. On my way out, I ran into my neighbour, she said,

"Maybe we can talk, get some coffee?"

Yeah, right, when I thought her boyfriend was responsible for the hand.

I said,

"I'm on my way to the graveyard."

Rocked her, took her a moment to regroup.

"Someone died?"

I snapped,

"Have a wild guess? You think I take my daily stroll in the cemetery?"

Left her literally open-mouthed.

Good.

By the time I got to the graveyard, the Guards had left, a police tape was around the grave. Shiv was standing beside it, a forlorn figure in the lightly pouring rain. I went to her, and she collapsed into my arms.

I don't know what I said but managed to utter some comfort banalities.

"Why?"

She asked me,

"Why would someone do such a thing?"

I said that I'd find them and there would be the devil to pay.

We left the cemetery, and I took her into Park House hotel, got her a large brandy and a Jay (double) for myself.

She drank quickly, shuddered then asked for another.

I could do that.

And did.

Blame the drink and or maybe thank it. We ended up at my apartment and the next morning, I woke to a sense of wonder. I didn't have a hangover; I did have a glorious woman in my bed.

I was making coffee when the doorbell went.

Oh fuck, if only I hadn't answered.

I opened the door to Rachel, she brushed past me, saying,

"I've decided to forgive you."

At that exact moment, Shiv emerged from the bedroom wearing my old blue Garda shirt that fell to her knees. Rachel stared at her, then to me,

"How come I never got to wear that shirt?"

I had no answer and to add injury to chaos, my neighbour came in bearing a cake, a peace gesture she kind of said, kind of in that she appeared stunned to see two women already in attendance. She spat,

"Sorry to interrupt your threesome."

Left the cake on the table, stormed out.

I managed to squeeze out,

"Thanks for the cake."

"Two criminals were crucified
On either side of Jesus.
One repented,
And was saved, do not despair.
The other didn't, do not presume."

—St. Augustine

26

For a moment after my neighbour left, Rachel, Shiv, and I stood in a mini frozen tableaux, then Rachel snorted, headed for the door, paused, looked at Shiv, said,

"That shirt makes you look fat."

And she was gone.

Shiv was silent for a moment then gulped,

"What a bitch."

Then she asked,

"Just how many women are you—"

Pause.

"—entertaining?"

After we had coffee, we took a walk toward Blackrock, climbed the tower of the diving boards, and looked out at Galway Bay.

Shiv glanced at me.

"You have such a look of almost peace."

I told the truth, said,

"Every time, the ocean makes me feel such a yearning."

She asked,

"For what?"

I said,

"I still don't know."

Later in the day, we had dinner in the Galleon. The owner, Ger, made a big fuss over us and put us in the window table.

"And another woman in the life of Jack Taylor."

I ordered steak, needed protein with all the women currently appearing in my befuddled existence. Shiv was about to order garlic bread and mushrooms as a starter, paused, asked,

"Will we be kissing later?"

I was a bit abashed but rallied with,

"Garlic gives a nice kick."

She went with the garlic.

Shiv lived in Dublin, worked for a PR firm and said she would need to leave the next day, asked,

"Will I be coming back?"

I had no hesitation.

"The sooner the better."

I still had to tell her that her brother was dead because he was doing a job for me, well, a theft in fact. Coward that I was, I kept putting it off, I now figured I might be able to put it better over the phone when she was back in Dublin.

Who was I kidding?

I was at the nun's convent again, led by the small, cute nun to the Mother Superior's office. Therese was behind her desk, and I handed over a large package. Her face lit up like a child at Christmas. She took the wrapping off to reveal the cross.

She gushed,

"Oh my God, you retrieved it, thank you a hundredfold."

Would I tell her the man who got it was thrown from a roof, his right hand severed?

No.

Let the moment shine unblemished.

She reached in her desk, took out a fat envelope, said,

"Such is my faith in you, I had this prepared."

I said,

"Please use it to help somebody."

She seemed uncertain so I added,

"The man who found the cross would wish that."

She put the envelope aside, asked,

"A wee dram to celebrate?"

I said,

"No; thank you, but I need a clear head."

Then I stood, added,

"I'm glad to have helped."

She looked like she might hug me, but I moved fast, wished her the best, and got out of there, feeling like shite.

I met with Jesse in Freeney's, an old-fashioned pub at the top of Quay Street. They have fishing tackle in the window; it's comforting in an old-school fashion. Inside, it's a no-frills pub, go elsewhere for your craft beers.

I knew Tom the barman from way back.

Jesse was seated at a table and Tom said to me,

"That kid is waiting for you."

Jesse was dressed in semi-goth, the dark clothes but easy on the kohl eye stuff. Tom might have suggested that he was in the wrong venue. I sat opposite him, he looked rough, bloodshot eyes and a slight tremor in his body. Drink was never his gig, his condition was about the death of Jordan.

He said,

"I don't drink alcohol, but I need something."

I ordered boilermakers, Tom raised an eyebrow but said nothing. I brought the drinks over, said to Jesse,

"Get that in you and we'll talk then."

He sank the Jay, then chased it with a swipe of the Guinness. I watched the booze work its dark magic, fast on the stomach of a novice. His face turned crimson, and his eyes lit up. He exhaled,

"Wow."

He said,

"I might get used to that."

I said,

"Don't."

He seemed to relax as the boilermaker weaved its spectral alchemy.

I said,

"I'm truly sorry you ever got involved in the whole security crash down. You did a cracker job; Jordan was delighted with you. What happened after, the horror of it is not on you. That's my burden."

He considered this, then,

"I wanted to go to the funeral, but I thought Benson's goons would be watching the mourners."

"You did the right thing."

I produced an envelope, said,

"Here's your slice of the job."

He recoiled,

"I'm a goth, can't take blood money."

"Don't be a fucking prima donna; that's my money."

He appeared suitably chastened, took the envelope, said,

"What I want is revenge, biblical type."

I said,

"Funny you should say that."

April 4, Trump brought before the court on thirty-four charges. Trump urged his followers to protest wildly. He predicted that death and destruction would follow if he was convicted.

In North Korea, the lunatic was still test-firing nuclear rockets.

Ireland was in turmoil with the ban on evictions being lifted. People were so incensed that the government might yet fall, like the water charges had brought down the last lot. Evictions were too dark an echo of our terrible past.

Joe Biden was due to visit Ireland the next week and already thirty-five alleged relatives had been found.

France was in its third week of the refuse workers' strike because the retirement age was being raised from sixty-two to sixty-four. Huge piles of garbage lined the streets with the lure of rats being imminent. Macron was in China, hoping to appease the Chinese threat of supplying weapons to Russia.

Today was Good Friday and indeed there was fuck-all good to be ascertained.

A guy had asked me if we didn't eat meat on that day when I was child. I said,

"We didn't eat meat until I was eighteen; not a religious or vegan gig, simply poverty."

Over a strong cup of coffee, I muttered a mangled line of the Leonard Cohen song.

There's a crack in the world,

Where the light gets in.

I wished that were so with my befuddled heart.

"In Ireland, we don't really
Adhere to the tradition
Of painting eggs.
What we do paint
Is the town
Red."

27

Jesse came to my apartment, carrying a bottle of Jay. Must be in the water but everybody who called on me brought a bottle of Jay.

Was I complaining?

Fuck no.

He was dressed in his habitual black, with a Willie Nelson bandana. His eyes were bloodshot. But he had a dark energy coming off him. I made coffee and saw him give the Jay a longing glance.

I said,

"Drink your coffee."

He did.

He asked if he could smoke, then rolled an expert handmade. Took a deep drag.

"I've been thinking how we might bury Benson."

I said,

"Basically, I want to go and bury my hurly in his face."

He smiled at that image, then,

"I've been working on a new multivirus, named it Edge. And if I can streamline it, it would wipe out all his resources."

I liked the sound of that, liked it a lot.

He continued,

"I've had to enlist two other hackers and we're nearly there. If it works, and I think it will, his various business, holdings, assets will—*puff*—disappear."

He blew out a perfect smoke ring, watched it dissipate.

In a previous case, I had been named in a will that gave me a large farm and a shitload of money. I was dangerously close to being wealthy.

I said,

"Money is no object."

He was surprised, said,

"No offence Jack, but I always thought you hadn't a pot to piss in."

"That used to be indeed the case, but, you know, the worm turns."

I got up, wrote out a sizable cheque, handed it to him. He exclaimed,

"Holy shit."

He stood up, excited, said,

"We're going to nail this fucker."

GALWAY'S EDGE

The next day, I was watching Sky News. The Chinese were right on the border of Taiwan, full military force on display. The US said they would supply Taiwan with weapons. To say the tension was high would be understatement.

I sipped my coffee, watched as the world turned yet another chapter of hate and aggression.

The doorbell went. I expected Jesse.

What I got was Father Richard, all twenty stone of him.

He was wearing a bright red shirt over black pants and shoes; a tan raincoat failed to disguise his girth. He asked,

"Might I come in?"

"You didn't bring a bottle?"

He looked puzzled. I said,

"Never no mind, come in."

He plonked himself on the sofa, pulled a well-worn briefcase onto his knees.

"I bear good news and a request."

"Always with the requests. What's the good news?"

He gave a wide smile, opened the briefcase, took out a roll of what appeared to be vellum, a manuscript. He said,

"Jack Taylor, you have been enrolled in the church's league of honour."

Seriously?

I asked,

"What does that mean?"

He sighed, taken aback at my less-than-delighted response. He said,

"It means the church recognizes the work, service, and duty you have provided to mother church."

I asked,

"Does it include a cash reward?"

He allowed a flash of irritation to show, snapped,

"Not everything is money."

"Tell that to the church."

He placed the vellum on the table.

"Very few people have received such an honour."

I let that float then said,

"I don't want it."

He asked,

"Can I have a drink?"

I poured him a Jay. I had enough supplies of it, God knows.

He took a large gulp, then,

"You are a grave disappointment to me, Jack."

"Tell me, seriously, what on earth will that piece of paper mean to my life?"

He shook his head.

"It gives a degree of honour to your life."

I let that slide.

I asked,

"You said there was a request?"

"Might I have a cigarette?"

I said,

"You're not shy about asking for stuff."

I had a pack of Major, the seriously hard-core brand that kicks you right in the face. Gave him one, and he lit it with a box of Swan matches, like my dad used to use. I had a moment of loss, then refocused on Richard. He drew deep on the cig, then blew out a near-perfect smoke ring.

It seemed to settle on him, and in turn, eased him some.

He began,

"Have you come across a priest named Father Frank Renton?"

I hadn't.

Said,

"No."

Richard took a deep sigh, then,

"Frank has the parish in Lower Salthill, not the large church, an adjacent one. He's young and full of breeze, ablaze with charisma. He is attracting young people through social media; he's on TikTok, which seems to be the site of choice. Somehow he's made himself a cool dude."

I said,

"Seems like he is just what the church badly needs."

He looked right at me, his eyes had that fervent glint, he said,

"But."

"There is always a but with matters religious."

He considered how much to reveal, went with,

"There have been three allegations of—"

He paused.

"—child abuse."

The church's dreaded words.

My heart sank. I asked,

"And what is it you think I can do?"

"Discredit them."

I asked,

"If they turn out to be true?"

He took a long time to answer, waved his glass for a refill. He didn't get one. He finally said,

"Bury them."

"The Galway Edge is
A form of twisted diplomacy.
First,
They pat your head.
Then,
They kick your arse."

28

I decided to pay Father Frank a visit. I checked the times of masses and figured I'd catch him after the noon one.

Mid-April, it was bitterly cold still and I had a brisk walk to Salthill. Mass was concluding as I arrived at the church. Lots of people, so Richard was right when he said Frank was very popular.

I waited while he had words with the emerging congregation, gave me a chance to observe him. He was in his early forties, thick brown hair, a strong face, and was tall in a slender frame. Even from a distance, he exuded an energy and the people he spoke to seemed lit up by him.

Finally, I approached him, asked,

"Father, if I might have a word?"

He gave me a long, calculating look then asked,

"Who are you?"

His voice was deep, trace of a British accent.

"I'm Jack Taylor, Father Richard sent me."

His face darkened.

"The church's hatchet man."

I said,

"I have an order of merit from the church, does that count?"

He gave a bitter laugh,

"Are they still peddling those nonsense things?"

He turned on his heel, said,

"Come on, it's time for my coffee."

Led me into a small bungalow beside the church, took off his vestments to reveal track gear underneath, gear that looked new and expensive.

The house was full of books, on every surface, overflowing from bookshelves, in piles on the floor, and a quick scan showed everything from philosophy through poetry to history.

He asked,

"Coffee?"

I agreed and he fired up one of those Nespresso machines. Fussed about in a small kitchen, said,

"I had biscuits, but the housekeeper probably stole them."

He put two steaming mugs on a coffee table.

"She steals all sorts of things."

I didn't know if he was serious, so I said,

"Maybe get a new one."

He gave me a look of incredulity, asked,

"And fire a sinner?"

Is there an answer to that, one that requires a measure of sanity? I said,

"Speaking of sin, you are no doubt aware of the allegations against you."

He took a long slug of coffee, then, energised anew, he near spat,

"Altar boys. I caught them stealing the wine so naturally they want to hurt me."

"Seems everybody is thieving from you."

He checked to see if I was being sarcastic.

He said,

"My weakness, if indeed weakness it be, is I have too big a heart."

I tried not to grimace, went with,

"I'll talk to the boys."

His face literally went purple with rage. He snarled,

"You most certainly will not, I forbid you, let it fade away."

I echoed,

"You forbid me?"

He gritted his teeth.

"You're a lapdog for some troublemakers in the church. They resent my popularity; they should be down on their knees thanking me for the good I'm doing."

I put the coffee down, said,

"I'll be in touch."

I reached the door and he warned,

"Don't be fooled by my apparent affability, I'm not the type of man to cross."

I nearly laughed.

"Sounds like a threat."

He smiled, answered,

"It's a promise."

I figured I'd take a run at the three boys in the frame. Not meetings I was keen on doing. I mean, am I going to say,

"I'm here to see if your son is a liar?"

Phew-oh.

Plus, I had no official standing.

I didn't think my order of merit would do me much good. I dressed in what I hoped would be a nonthreatening fashion. Chinos, white shirt, and a rowing club tie I'd bought in Oxfam. A dark blazer from the same outlet almost fit me if I rolled up the sleeves. I studied my own self in the mirror.

I looked like a dodgy insurance clerk whose best years were long gone.

The first family were the Devlins; they lived in Shantalla. Their house was a two storey, with a front garden, recently tended; it had rows of daffodils, roses, and an apple tree. My heart was hammering in my chest. I rang the bell.

The door opened to a woman in her late forties, tall with dark hair scraped back into a severe bun. Her face was free of makeup and her eyes looked wounded. I said,

"Mrs. Devlin, I'm very sorry to trouble you. I wonder if I might talk to you about Ronan?"

Her face morphed to rage.

"Who sent you?"

Was I going to tell the truth and say the church? Was I, fuck.

I said,

"I'm here on behalf of a man who wants to see your son gets justice."

She debated that then stood aside.

"Come in."

The house was tidy, all the surfaces clean, no sign that a boy lived there. I asked,

"Is your husband home?"

She sighed, the type that rises from the very depth of your core.

"My husband had decided that the way to handle this business is to drink, as if he could wash away the whole sordid affair."

I said,

"I'm very sorry."

She nodded, asked,

"Would you like some tea?"

I wouldn't, but it is a small way of breaking the tension, so I said that would be great. She busied herself doing that while I looked at a framed photo of what I presumed was the family. They were all smiling and the sun backlit the picture. The sun would not shine on them again.

She brought in a small tray, with a plate of fruitcake. Poured two cups of tea, handed me one with a plate holding the cake. That fucking cake near broke my heart. I sipped at the tea, tried a small nibble of the cake.

I said,

"I met with the priest, Father Frank."

She grimaced and a slight tremor shook her hand. She had to put the cup down. She asked,

"What do you make of him?"

I told the truth, I said,

"He is a narcissistic arsehole."

She gave a tiny laugh, surprised herself.

"You're very direct."

I asked,

"Might I meet Ronan?"

Her face fell in on itself, as if all the vitality were drained from it. She said,

"He locks himself in his room, I must bring his meals to him. He was such an active lad before, out the door at every opportunity. But now . . ."

She trailed off.

A silence fell, I had nothing to say. She said,

"I'd love to kill that priest, feed my rage, it is all that keeps me going. I've lost my family."

I stood up, thanked her for her hospitality. She asked,

"What will you do?"

"I will do my very best to take down Frank."

She touched my arm, said,

"Thank you."

Oh fuck.

"I'm something
Else."

29

The second woman on my list of three opened the door and I went into my spiel about the church. She slapped my face, hard, and banged the door shut.

Not a church person then.

I figured I'd leave the third family until the next day. My face felt burnt, from the slap, but mainly from shame.

Go figure.

I headed home, opened my door to find a large bald man sitting on my sofa. He was dressed in an impressive black suit, like silk maybe, a muted red tie, and highly polished black shoes. His body screamed muscle, hard muscle, not the gym type. He weighed, I guessed, round two hundred pounds.

"I'm Kane."

I stared at him, asked,

"Why are you sitting in my apartment? I could shoot you and have probable cause."

He laughed, said,

"You'd need a big gun."

Christ.

I poured myself a Jay and even offered him a shot.

He said,

"I don't drink."

Course not.

I leaned against my back wall, asked,

"What do you want?"

He flexed his fingers, a cracking noise, then he smiled, said,

"I wanted to introduce myself. I'm the new head of security for Mr. Benson. As you undoubtedly know, his premises were recently burgled; I'm to ensure it won't happen again. As you seem to be the local clarion of information, I think you should spread the word. Mr. Benson feels that somehow you had a hand in that event."

He chuckled.

"A hand on the grave, so to speak."

He let that sink in, then stood up, said,

"You have, as they say, been cautioned."

He was at the door. I said,

"Do I look chastised?"

He considered that, then lashed out with a right fist, straight into my gut. I doubled up, fell to my knees. He said,

"You do now."

He bent down, grabbed my hair, hauled my face up to meet his eyes. I saw black orbs of nothingness. He snarled,

"You've met all kinds of crazies, psychos, nut jobs, but know this—"

He paused, then,

"—I'm something else."

I met with Jesse in Jury's bar at the bottom of Quay Street. It's the kind of bar you can nigh guarantee you won't run into anyone you know.

Jesse was rocking his goth look, kohl eyes, dark jeans, dark jacket. The barman gave him a look.

Jesse said,

"Not a goth-friendly venue."

It was early and we were drinking coffee. Jesse said,

"I could kill a pint."

I told him about Kane.

About him being the hatchet guy for Benson.

He listened carefully, asked,

"The stomach punch, did it hurt?"

I said,

"Like a bastard, still does."

Jesse said,

"Fuck it, I'm having a drink,"

He went to the bar, got two Jays. I said,

"I hope that's one each."

He smiled, said,

"Sláinte amach."

The drink hit him fast, reddened his cheeks, the kohl around his eyes highlighting the effect. He said,

"Benson, we need to kill that bollix."

I took a deep breath.

"I think we should call off the blitz on him."

Jesse stared at me, gulped.

"After what he did to Jordan, no way am I letting that slide; if you're out, I'll do it my own self."

I said,

"I'm trying to protect you; these are people who throw somebody off a building, then sever his hand and put it on his grave for his sister to find."

He shook his head.

"Somebody has to hold that fuck responsible."

I caved, said,

"Okay then, but you have to leave the city right after. I'll contact you when the coast clears."

"What does that mean, the coast being clear?"

"I'm going after Kane."

"And here where our graves will be greening
Just smile and be happy again.
We point . . . to a name on a cross."

—Robert W. Service

Jerry Springer dies on April 27 at the age of seventy-nine.

Joe Biden declares he will run in the next election.

Trump, facing new multiple charges of sexual assault, mocks Biden for going to Ireland in a time of national crisis.

The next day, he announces he will fly to visit his Doonbeg golf course in Ireland the following Wednesday.

30

I'm sitting on Eyre Square watching the crew of Afghan refugees gathered in blankets.

A man approaches, he is dressed in a very expensive cashmere coat, more striking in contrast to the Afghans' blankets. He has silver hair in abundance, beautifully cut Italian loafers I recognise from an ad I saw in *GQ* magazine when I was at the dentist, and yes, those loafers have silly tassels.

His face is tanned, and he bears a striking to Russell Crowe.

He stops, asks,

"Jack Taylor?"

I nod and he asks if he may sit.

Sure.

I smell strong cologne from him. He says,

"I have done extensive research on you."

I ask the obvious,

"Why?"

He takes a deep breath; it gives off a blend of mint mouthwash.

He falters, then,

"I want you to kill me."

Déjà vu.

A priest, Father Malachy, was a friend of my horrendous mother. After her passing (thank God), he becomes the bane of my life, forever conjoining me into doing favours for him and the church. He was diagnosed with aggressive cancer that would kill him not only slowly but horribly.

He couldn't kill himself due to his church's stance on suicide, so he wanted me to do the deed.

It was the time of what I think of as my "falcon case" and events near broke me; I went on an almighty bender and when I surfaced a week later, Malachy was dead.

By his own hand?

I didn't ask.

He had always scoffed at my predilection for crime fiction but on his bedside table was a copy of Elmore Leonard's *City Primeval*.

Go figure.

The usual trite Irish lies were said of him.

He had a good heart. He didn't.

He meant well. Never.

He cared for the poor. Not for a moment.

The man holds out his hand, says,

"I'm Peter Bird. I know it's a big ask, but I gather from the data on the Internet that you're not a stranger to violence."

This was not flattery. I said,

"Don't believe what you read; it says too that I'm a dangerous man."

That rocked him a little, but he rallied.

"That's what I need, a man accustomed to danger."

I thought, *let's state the obvious*, asked,

"Why do you want to die?"

He swallowed.

"May I sit?"

I waved a hand and he sat, keeping a respectable distance from me. He reached in his jacket, took out a pack of Marlboro Red, the soft pack like you can get in the US. He offered me one, I took it, and he produced a heavy gold Zippo.

I love those lighters. They fuel my love of the States. He lit us up, then closed the lighter with that great heavy clunk. He said,

"I had finally given up smoking but now that I'm going to die—"

Paused.

"—with your valued assistance, it seems I can smoke like a lunatic."

He smoked for a bit, then,

"I'm fifty-three years of age, I'm rich, with no family, but the doctors have diagnosed me with a very nasty virulent cancer that is going to kill me in a slow, lengthy fashion. My birthday is coming up and I'd like to die on that day."

He reached in his jacket again, took out a thick envelope, left it on the seat between us, said,

"There's ten thousand euro in there."

I didn't touch the money, asked,

"How do you want to die?

"Gun

"Rope

"Strangled

"Carbon monoxide?

"And pills are a nice cushy way to check out."

He said,

"On my birthday, I'll be alone in my house, and I want to be dead before noon. I'll let you decide on the means, nothing too painful."

I said,

"Okay."

He was kind of shocked.

"How do I know you won't just keep the money and do nothing?"

I smiled, said,

"You don't."

He got up to leave, said,

"Well, that's it then."

I said,

"Give me the lighter and cigs."

He asked,

"Why?"

"I want to touch base with my love of America."

He handed them over reluctantly.

I stood up, said,

"See you on your birthday."

"Down Galway's crooked streets
A man
Must walk.
Who is not, his own self,
Completely crooked?"

—Jack Taylor, 2023

31

There is a German-Chechen named Gustav. Time back, the light of his life, his daughter named Lisa-bell, was taken by a notorious paedophile. The Guards came up empty.

I did the round of known sex offenders. You know the streets as I do, you know these creatures, or at least where they congregate. I brought my hurly and within two days, I found the girl.

Gustav, as hard a man as I've ever known, cried, mumbled,

"Anything, anytime, you want anything Jack, 'tis done."

I found him now in Fahy's pub, a pub supposedly closed but open to a certain element. I was included in that circle. It was where dark matters were dark dealt with.

Gustav was sitting at a table in the back, playing backgammon with a crew of granite-faced men. Gustav was dressed in one of those black leather jackets from Eastern Europe, almost like a uniform with these guys. He was in his fifties and his nose had been sliced down the middle with a fishhook; it made him look like a malevolent hawk. His face carried other scars, but his grey eyes carried a look that in a certain light almost seemed empathetic. That was misleading.

He stood, hugged me tight. Not many men have ever hugged me. I'm not the type. He spoke to one of his crew who produced a bottle of Raki, a shot glass, he poured for me. He said, I think,

"Rostropovich."

I drank it in one and phew-oh, it burned like acid, my eyes watered and my chest felt like it had been hit with a sledgehammer. He asked,

"What do you need, my brother?"

I said,

"A heavy gun, ammunition."

Didn't faze him. He barked at another of the crew, who got up and left the pub. Gustav offered another drink and I said,

"God, no, I won't be able to walk."

He laughed.

"Why we drink it."

His man came back, carrying an oilcloth, put it on the table, then stood to block any view of our business. Gustav unwrapped the cloth to reveal a very large, heavy gun. He whistled, said,

"This is a Colt Anaconda steel revolver and it takes .44 magnum cartridge, it weighs nearly five pounds, it shoots thirteen rounds, which I think should be enough for whatever you're hunting."

Hunting!

No point in trying to snow Gustav.

He added,

"Whatever animal you're after, this will blow a hole as big as a fist, and if you aim for centre mass, you'll blast the heart across a room. I've added a Taser in case you want them to dance."

I passed a thick envelope across the table, and he waved it away. I said,

"For your little girl, take her to that Disney place in Florida."

I took the gun, pushed it in the back of my jeans; it felt cold, heavy, and lethal.

Good.

The Taser I put in my jacket, maybe surprise the busker who sang the same song endlessly.

I reached in my jacket, took out the Zippo and the cigs, said,

"A small reminder of me."

He flicked the Zippo, listened to the thunk as he closed it down, said,

"I love that music."

A man after my own heart.

Here's the odd thing, having parted with the cigs, I felt a massive desire for one, so I went into Brendan Holland, asked for a pack of the mule kick, Major. Brendan looked at me.

He said,

"Try the vapes."

My face registered my disdain, but he was not a man to be easily sidetracked; he said,

"Two hundred thousand people have stopped smoking because of vaping; try this one."

It was a small blue plastic item with the name Lost Mary.

I said,

"Lost Mary?"

He laughed, said,

"Me neither."

I asked how you worked the bloody thing.

He said,

"Put the tiny funnel on the top in your mouth—"

He paused, then,

"—and you just suck."

I was sitting in my apartment, the Anaconda before me. It looked deadly.

I was still heartsick about the death of Jordan and the severing of his hand made my guts churn. I had no doubt it was Kane who did it.

Jesse had provided lots of information on him.

All bad.

When Jesse finally took down all Benson's enterprises, there was no doubt that Kane would target Jesse and then me. Here's the thing, Kane lived in Nun's Island, in Altenagh House, where I had lived. I still had the keys.

Kane's routine was to do whatever bad shite he performed for Benson and get home about eleven each night.

There is a cold, dark part of my soul where revenge and guilt intertwine. I went there now, and slowly loaded the gun, thirteen shining shells.

Three days later I let myself into the grounds of Altenagh. Hid in the shrubbery by the gated entrance and, sure enough, come eleven a BMW roared along. Kane got out, didn't look around; in his mind, he was the one who attacked people.

I gave him half an hour to get settled then let myself in, climbed the stairs to number 16. I could hear music from inside, sounded like Metallica.

I knocked on the door and he opened it, I put the gun right in his face and moved him back into the apartment. He was more shocked than alarmed, then his natural aggression took over and he scoffed,

"What? You going to shoot me, a has-been drunk, you haven't the balls."

I shot him three times in the chest.

And Gustav was right, it did blow out his heart, right across the room.

Brid Nolan was an Irish shaman.
She said,
"Murder
Leads to an edge of
Disintegration
Of the heart,
An edge
Of
Withering of the soul."
1948–2003

32

Anne Perry died, the bed of heaven to her. She was eighty-four. She wrote over one hundred books and her history included her and her friend Pauline beating Pauline's mother to death with a brick.

Forty times they'd hit her.

Her story was filmed as *Heavenly Creatures*, introducing an eighteen-year-old Kate Winslet.

May 3: Trump arrives for twenty-four hours to visit his hotel in Doonbeg.

I was coming out of the Protestant Church St. Nicholas, when a Bohermore woman passed me. She greeted,

"Hiya, Loveen."

The Galway greeting that is truly old school.

Karl Lagerfeld died, and the Met Ball in New York celebrated his life with a truly outrageous display of black and white fashion. Lagerfeld once said,

"I don't like standard beauty, there is no beauty without strangeness."

So, no surprise that he left 1.2 million to his cat.

Not a dog lover, I guess.

The media was ablaze on the murder of Kane.

Did I feel any remorse?

Like fuck.

I went to see the Mother Superior, Therese.

I needed to talk to someone. My life was in such a state of bewilderment, and I'd literally blown somebody away. So once again I was in Nun's Island.

The same small young cheerful nun answered the heavy door, exclaimed,

"Mr. Taylor, again!"

I asked,

"Might the Mother Superior see me?"

She gave a radiant smile, said,

"She's with a priest but he'll be gone soon."

I asked,

"How do you know?"

She laughed.

"She never spends long with the clergy."

There were so many ironies in that sentence.

I went into Therese's office, she rose to greet me, said,

"I nearly hugged you."

I had no reply to that.

She said,

"I'll get you a glass of Jameson."

Good Lord, how tight was I with the nuns?

I said,

"I'm boycotting that since they decided to reestablish supplies to Russia."

She smiled in a slightly puzzled way, asked,

"Some coffee? I've got the Nespresso."

"Sounds good."

She got the coffee organised and put two mugs and a plate of cookies on the desk.

"Milk?"

"No, black please."

She said,

"No surprise there."

She took a sip of hers, went,

"Ahh."

She sat back.

"What's troubling you, Jack?"

"I look troubled?"

She stared at me, said,

"It's in your eyes."

I said,

"I want to run a scenario by you."

Therese never ceased to take me from left field and now, again, she stunned me by referencing Leonard Cohen,

"Everything is cracked,

"So the light gets in."

She had the quote not quite like L. C. wrote it, but was I going to be pedantic?

Nope.

She added,

"So, the scenario?"

Phew-oh.

I began,

"A man I know, his treasured friend was not only murdered, but his grave desecrated, and the killer mocked the man; so if that man took biblical vengeance, would that be, like, a sin?"

She was silent as she considered the question, finally she said,

"Don't do it, Jack, it will murder your own soul."

I had nothing so offered nothing.

She opened a drawer in her desk, took out a small phial, said,

"This is holy water from Medjugorje, it will bring some modicum of peace."

Yeah, right.

I took it from politeness more than anything else.

"Thank you, and thank you for listening to me."

She asked, concern warm in her voice,

"Did I help you?"

I stood up, headed for the door, turned, said,

"No, you didn't."

I headed down the town and stopped at the Salmon Weir Bridge and, with all my might, flung the phial into the wild river.

I sneered,

"*Vaya con Dios.*"

As I watched a salmon leap, my heart too, I remembered lines from Don Winslow's *City on Fire.*

> The nuns used to say that the devil comes disguised as
> an angel.
> That the worst things you'll do, you'll do for the best
> reasons.
> The most hateful things you do, you'll do for the ones
> you love most.

"Jack says
The great Leonard Cohen
Had some lines
That you need a break in the state of the world.
Otherwise,
No way
Can any light sneak in."

33

Father Frank!

I had considered various scenarios to stop his child molesting.

My lethal friend Gustav had said,

"Anything you want, it's done."

So I called him, told him about the priest, he listened, then,

"How much damage do you want us to administer?"

I said,

"Enough that he doesn't hurt any more children."

Gustav was silent until,

"My lieutenant, Vladmir, was abused by a priest. I will send him."

I was smart enough not to ask what the action might be.

But it already sounded biblical.

The Guards came on the 6th of May.

The day Prince Charles was finally coronated as king.

I didn't think the two events were connected.

They nearly broke down the door. I was in nigh coma after a night of booze. Since I was boycotting Jameson, which I am sure didn't rattle any of the producers, I had decided to try out as many American labels as I could think of.

I had begun with Maker's Mark and alas, I overdrank. I shouted at the door,

"Hold on a frigging minute."

Pulled on my 501s, pair of Skechers slip-ons, and a battered, faded T-shirt with the logo,

Saw Doctors.

Love that band.

Six Garda, led by a bully known as Ford; we had history, all of it bad. He shoved paper in my face, snarled,

"This is a search warrant for a weapon."

The Anaconda of course.

It was hidden in oilskin near the Blackrock diving board. I have my moments.

They found nothing but turned the apartment upside down. I stayed in the kitchen, sipping coffee. When they were done, Ford got right in my face, snarled,

"I'll be watching, Taylor, sooner or later you'll fuck up."

"His eyes fixed on the horizon,

On the distant image

Of New Orleans in the mist.

He was trying to make out once again the dancer

In the mirage.

But

All he could see now

Was a swirl of dust,

Sunrays and dew."

—Ray Celestin
The Axeman's Jazz

34

The time was coming when we'd take down Benson. Jesse called me and said the virus was near complete. Jesse advised that I should get out of the city when it went down.

For a long time, I'd been planning on visiting New Orleans.

The books of

Ray Celestin,

James Lee Burke,

John Connolly

Had sparked the dream in me.

I wanted

Beignets with my coffee,

Music on Bourbon Street,

Po'boy sandwiches,

Crayfish.

The David Simon series *Treme* sealed the deal.

I went to Annette Hynes and arranged to travel on the day after I was due to shoot the man on his birthday.

The Anaconda was back in my apartment. I took it apart, cleaned it, dry fired it.

Lock and load.

Good to go.

The next few days, I tried to literally let my breath out. I have always found calm, solace, and comfort in books. When my mind is on fire and I'm not quelling it with booze, I rely on books.

I went to see Vinny in Charlie Byrne's Bookshop and Leon in Dubray.

Got

Dennis Lehane, *Small Mercies*,

Fernanda Melchor, *This Is Not Miami*,

Don Winslow, *City on Fire*,

Ray Celestin, *Jazz Quartet*.

Then went to McCambridge's, which was no longer the family business, more's the Irish pity, bought by the Musgrave group.

Bought a bottle of sour mash, keep the New Orleans gig hopping.

Back at my apartment, I added the books to my shelf. My plan was to read for a few days and, as the kids say, "just chill."

35

A knock at the door and I opened it to Shiv. She looked terrific and was I glad to see her?

You betcha.

She had a suede jacket, with a white T-shirt, faded blue jeans, Converse sneakers. Looking good.

We hugged and I felt stirrings, thank God. She'd brought a bottle of Jay and I didn't mention my small boycott of it.

She came in and, out of the blue, I asked,

"Wanna come to New Orleans?"

She gave a delighted laugh, said,

"Can we have a coffee first?"

Thus began one of the best few days of my tattered life.

We did all the Galway things.

Ate oysters in Moran's of the Weir.

Fed the swans.

Hired a car and cruised Connemara.

Went to the Burren.

Went to the Cliffs of Moher.

Took a voyage on a Galway hooker, the boat, not a working girl. There is also a Galway beer named after this wonderful craft.

Took a shitload of photos.

I see these snaps now and my heart pines.

We spent a night on Inishmore, the largest of the Aran islands.

Sailing across Galway Bay on a fine sunny day, you could believe the world sometimes tilted in a glorious way.

Back in the city, I was highlighting to Shiv the best episodes of *The Last of Us.*

We were drinking hot toddies and for some insane reason, I opted to tell her of the events leading up to her brother Jordan's death. The whiskey had loosened my tongue and any bit of sense I possessed.

Shiv listened with an expression of horror, and when I was finished, she let out the softest sigh I ever heard. She asked,

"You sent him to steal from that lunatic?"

I nodded, tried,

"I never anticipated that Benson would have Jordan killed."

She murmured,

"Anticipated?"

Then she slapped my face, hard, said,

"Fuck you."

"To drive away
A woman
Who might be
In love with you
Is the very edge
Of madness."

36

There is a guy named Troy with a very odd upbringing. Born in Galway, his parents moved to South Boston when he was a child. He grew up in Southie, the Bohermore of Boston, learned all about poverty and rage.

In his fifties, he won 100,000 on the lottery.

He returned to Galway and bought a small, run-down pub close to the train station and named it Dorchester, the birthplace of his hero, Dennis Lehane.

The pub was modelled on the pubs of Southie, even had a jukebox.

The walls were festooned with an American flag and posters of Bobby Sands, John F. Kennedy, and some pope. Republican songs littered the jukebox.

He loved the Galway swans and because I'd stopped a swan killer, he believed I could do no wrong.

Sigh.

Came bearing gifts.

He poured me a pint, asked,

"Jameson?"

I said,

"No, a shot of Paddy."

I handed him the parcel. He said,

"A present, it's been 1958 since anybody gave me anything but grief."

He unwrapped the paper, a book, looked at the title,

Small Mercies, by Dennis Lehane.

His face lit up, he exclaimed,

"The new one?"

I said,

"Maybe his best since *Mystic River*."

He put the book on the shelf, said,

"I had a terrific dog, a rescue. He was stolen last week; there's a gang of arseholes stealing dogs to order, you think you might be able to help?"

I said I'd try, and he asked,

"You still have your hurly?"

I nodded and he wrote down some names, said,

"The ones who took Blitz, they are two brothers, aged eighteen and nineteen, they live in a fine house in Taylor's Hill; Daddy gave it to them. Stealing dogs is a rush for them, Eddie and Tom Fletcher."

He surveyed me, asked,

"How's your love life?"

I told the truth.

"Broken."

He mused on that then reached for a bottle off the top shelf.

"Glenfiddich, the silver ghost of whisky."

I liked that.

He poured two shots, said,

"Here's to reconciliation."

Amen.

I downed it in one, felt a lovely kick, said,

"'Tis class."

I said,

"Tell me about your dog."

His face lit up.

"Blitz is a German shepherd, he loves me to bits, he's a rescue dog; his former owner used to beat him with chains."

I felt the rage, asked,

"Did you track down that bollix?"

He smiled without any hint of humour, said,

"Oh yeah, I beat him with bicycle chains."

I asked,

"You know who took the dog, why didn't you take your chain and go get the dog yer own self?"

He sighed, said,

"The parents, they're business associates, they drink here, they are a large part of my trade."

I finished the drinks, stood, said,

"I'll get right on it."

He shook my hand, said,

"Thanks Jack, you're one of the best."

The weather was still unreasonably warm. I walked to town, gave a bad busker some bad money and he shouted,

"I take all the major credit cards."

For a wild moment I felt Shiv's hand in mine.

And my heart shrivelled anew.

37

I was in Garavan's, working on my first pint.

Just as I had decided on my next whisky, Owen Daglish slipped onto the stool beside me. He was dressed in an off-green linen suit, a lopsided dark tie, and, if I wasn't mistaken, Birkenstocks.

Surely not.

Ordered a pint for him and asked for a Teacher's.

Owen gasped, queried,

"Not the Jay?"

I gave him my tolerant smile, said,

"Because they reexported to Russia."

He sipped his pint.

"You'll have annoyed Putin."

What else was there to say other than,

"Good"?

He stared at the Teacher's, asked,

"How is it?"

I took a decent sup, said,

"Pretty okay."

We were silent for a while then I asked him,

"A linen suit, like seriously?"

He hand-smoothed the myriad creases.

"I had to be in court, I'm getting divorced."

Showstopper.

I tried,

"Sorry to hear that."

And I was.

A grim silence hovered until Owen ordered us another round. He said,

"I hear you had the Guards?"

I sighed, said,

"They didn't find anything."

The drinks came and Owen downed his shot, grimaced, said,

"They know you had some part in the killing of Benson's enforcer; stay focused, they aren't done with you yet."

I asked,

"Why would I kill him?"

He gave a low laugh, echoed,

"Why would you not?"

True.

I felt it was best not to push on that, asked,

"Do you know the Fletcher brothers?"

Nudging his pint, he asked,

"You going to shoot them too?"

Phew-oh.

A guy we both vaguely knew, in that I'd lent him money, approached, asked,

"Mind if I join ye lads?"

Owen, without turning, hissed,

"Fuck off."

Succinct.

Owen asked,

"Join me for a cig?"

I did.

We were outside, the sun was shining, another mini heat wave in these early days of May. Owen produced a pack of Carrolls, offered, I said,

"I'm vaping."

He growled,

"Don't be an ejit."

"What about them brothers?"

He flicked his cig high in the air, it landed near a refugee, who picked it up, got a few drags out of it.

"Those brothers like to hang out with the alt-right groups, harass the refugees, even burn out their tent encampments. They do a sideline in stealing dogs to order."

I asked,

"The Guards?"

He laughed, said,

"Their old man plays golf with the superintendent."

He then gave me the look, went,

"Ah, Jack, tell me you're not getting involved in this."

I finished my drink, said,

"What can I tell you, I love dogs."

Owen changed tack,

"I saw you with a fine-looking lass the other day."

The heart that skipped a beat.

I managed to croak,

"We're no longer together."

He pondered this, then,

"How would you feel about giving me her phone number?"

Seriously.

I snapped,

"You're in the midst of a divorce; I mean you have got to be kidding!"

He raised his eyebrows.

"But you're finished with her, right?"

I tried to damp down the hurt/rage building, asked,

"You think for a second I'm not hurting maybe?"

He laughed.

He fucking laughed.

"Aw, Jack, you don't give a shit about women; you're nearly always fucking up relationships."

"A hurly
Crafted from the best ash
Can have steel bands
Wired on the head
To add heft
And, indeed,
To give it
Edge."

38

The Fletcher brothers were playing frisbee in their front garden when I arrived. Dressed in track gear from the North Face, nothing but the best for them. They were blond, tall, and had a vibe that screamed entitlement.

I waited until the frisbee was midflight and moving fast, and I used the hurly to whack it out of the air. I connected just right, and it flew toward the house.

The taller of the two brothers, Tom, looked at me, snarled,

"The fuck do you think you're doing?"

The younger one was coming at me, his fists clenched, and I let him come to within a yard then swept his legs from under him with the hurly.

"I've come to collect the dog you stole."

Tom said,

"Go fuck yourself."

So I knocked him on his arse, said,

"We can do this all day; I need the workout."

Tom said,

"There are cages in the back."

I got the dog, he still had his name tag, then I called animal welfare to collect the others. I attached a leash to Blitz, walked over to the two brothers; both had got shakily to their feet. I said,

"Don't give me cause to return."

The taller one tried,

"Our father will deal with you."

"You do that, and he and you will be all over the papers. Dog-thief family, has a ring to it."

The housing crisis was way out of control, tent cities were springing up, and a camp in Dublin was firebombed by the antirefugee gang, a group of forty men, international refugees were literally dumped in a small village called Inch.

The locals set up a roadblock/barricade and were in a standoff with the Guards. More such barricades were threatened throughout the country.

And more than two hundred fifty people were arriving every day at Dublin Airport.

The government were suggesting floating hotels off the coast.

Like that was ever going to float!

DeSantis announced his bid for the Republican nomination. Musk, a supporter, gave him Twitter as a launching pad, but it was a disaster, twenty-five minutes of bleeps, silences, and meltdowns.

To the gleeful delight of Trump.

Anti-Putin Russian troops were rebelling against the Kremlin, which could only be good news for Ukraine.

Ireland was having a heat wave this 26th of May.

Five members of a family—father, mother, three sons—were charged with one hundred thirty sexual offences against other children in their family and found guilty. The details included rape and appalling abuse.

I stood on the diving tower of Blackrock, across the road from my apartment and asked,

"What happened to our country?"

We were still having a mini heat wave so Irish guys were leaping into cargo shorts and thick socks with heavy sandals to emphasise their whiteness, not a pretty sight.

Jesse came to the apartment, dressed like a citizen, his hair tidied, white shirt over chinos, a light fawn jacket. I said,

"You look almost normal."

He smiled,

"We are ready to rock."

Meaning the time had come to cripple Benson's business. Jesse said,

"I had four hackers helping me and we are launching a four-pronged assault on every aspect of his business. Took us two weeks to get every-thing in place. I have to say that Benson had state-of-the-art safeguards and firewalls of real excellence—"

Paused,

"—but we are better."

I handed him a fat envelope, covering the cost of the other hackers and a fine bonus. I had an extra ten grand to play with from the man who wanted me to kill him.

I asked,

"When will you leave?"

He laughed, said,

"Today; why I'm fronting the citizen gear."

I shook his hand.

"Thank you."

He said,

"To have Benson crash and burn, that's the joy."

And crash and burn Benson did.

Spectacularly.

The media were all over it, blaming the Russians.

Of course.

I was watching the drama unfold on TV when there was a knock on my door. My next-door neighbour. She looked distraught. I asked,

"Want to come in?"

She did.

Her appearance was haggard. Tangled hair, dark circles under her eyes, an off-white T-shirt, and baggy shorts. She gave me a pleading look, asked,

"Is it too early for a Jameson?"

I said,

"I don't have Jay anymore."

She sat edgily on a chair.

"He dumped me."

I figured that was Benson, dumping her along with his useless stock. Before I could form an answer, she continued,

"He is selling the apartment; I'll have nowhere to live."

I didn't feel any empathy. I tried,

"Don't you have family, friends you can stay with?"

She shook her head, said,

"Everyone disapproved of me and Benson."

No surprise but I tried for some feeling, asked,

"Because he is married?"

She near shrieked,

"Because he's an arsehole."

Well, no argument there.

She looked straight into my eyes, then,

"I know we may have got off to a shaky start, but I was thinking we could start over and it's not like I'd have far to move."

Ha.

I asked,

"Move in with me?"

She tried on a shy smile, looked like a sneer, said,

"I think we might surprise ourselves and find it's a rush."

Fuck me.

I acted as if I was considering it, and she held grimly to that smile, then I said,

"No."

Took her a time to fully grasp my answer, then,

"Might I ask why?"

I said,

"It's not complicated. I don't like you."

She left, trailing a string of obscenities including the description *dipso*, which kind of made me smile; she slammed the door and I went to the cupboard, took out a fresh bottle of Paddy, poured a dram, said,

"Here's to the dipso."

"When you live on
The edge,
The daily rush becomes
An addiction,
So that
A return to so-called
Normalcy
Is not even an option."

—Jesse, überhacker

39

Benson was arrested on a myriad of financial charges. Usually these high rollers, of whom we had near a litany, got to delay proceedings and hightailed it to America, but Benson was not even allowed bail.

I'd have emailed Jesse with the news, but he was deep under the radar, embedded off the grid.

Ukraine was launching missiles into Russia, had knocked out a tower block in the centre of Moscow. Russia responded with nigh 24/7 strikes on Kyiv. Russia accused the UK of supporting the Ukraine cause and as such, UK officials would be targets.

I was reviewing my life as it unfolded in the past weeks.

I had a contract to kill a man on his birthday. I checked the calendar; he had a few weeks to go yet.

Benson was gone.

His chief thug was history, and I felt no regret about him.

I had returned a dog to his owner and got to use the hurly on a pair of apprentice young arseholes.

I was managing to get by without my beloved Jameson. Of course, it meant I was journeying through the whiskey landscape. Every few days, a different brand.

A postcard arrived from the Cayman Islands with the wonderful, "Wish I was here."

It helped to be Irish to grasp the logic of that.

I got a summons from the Mother Superior. I wondered if she'd got me on speed dial. The heat wave on this June 4 was in full blaze so I put on a linen shirt I got from the charity shop. A pair of light canvas shoes and a pair of faded jeans that were nearly white from washing. If I had sunglasses, I could have perched them on my head and completed the whole trendy arsehole vibe.

At the convent, the same small nun greeted me,

"Mr. Taylor, always a joy."

Hmm.

Then she led me into Therese's office. Therese was allowing for the heat wave in so far as she was wearing a white shirt over navy skirt and, I swear, trainers. I said,

"You look almost human."

On reflection, that was a nasty comment and I instantly regretted it. Her face registered a fleeting film of hurt and I said,

"I don't really mean that."

She gave me a studied look, then,

"You meant it, Jack, it's your modus operandi to retaliate first."

Nailed.

I tried to slide past that with,

"No, the look suits you."

Too lame, too late.

Story of my life.

She came out from behind her desk, went to the cupboard, said,

"I know you're not drinking Jameson, but where do you stand on sherry?"

We skipped the sherry; I told her it was what Connemara men drank in Lent as penance. That amused her greatly.

I asked,

"What can I help you with?"

She took a deep breath, said,

"On Friday nights, dead cats are being left on our doorstep."

I said,

"Good lord. How many Fridays, or how many cats?"

"Three, all black cats and with their throats cut."

I did the requisite dance, asked,

"The Guards?"

She sighed, said,

"They've promised to investigate, but I feel they have more pressing concerns."

I asked,

"Any threats, unsavoury characters lurking around?"

She shook her head, said,

"Not for the first time, we have to rely on you, Jack Taylor."

I asked,

"Any idea of the time when the cats are, um, left?"

She said,

"It is never before eight and usually occurs around midnight and it has been a Friday each time."

She added,

"This is someone who doesn't like nuns."

I nearly laughed, said,

"He sure as hell doesn't like cats."

She reached beneath, produced a thick envelope, said,

"This is for your trouble."

Taking money from nuns?

No.

If it was a priest, I'd empty their wallet, but a nun, nope.

She pressed,

"Jack, this is your work, you can't not be paid."

I stood up, said,

"I'll set up vigil on Friday night, alert your flock not to panic if they see a man in the foliage close to the door."

Therese came round the desk and before I could stop her, she got me in a hug, she smelled of lilies and fresh linen.

A lump in my throat, I said,

"Right, I'll be off."

The little nun on the door gave me a lovely smile, said,

"We'd be lost without you, Mr. Taylor."

I walked toward town, feeling like a complete fraud.

"There was once a demographic
Survey done
To determine if money
Was connected to happiness and
Ireland
Was the only place
Where this did not
Turn out to be
True."

—Fiona Shaw

40

Friday, June 9, I prepared to go after the cat killer. I said that aloud and realised how weird it was. I wore a black sweatshirt, black 501s, dark shoes, and I'd have worn a watch cap, but the heat wave was keeping the temperature in the 20s degrees Celsius.

I was at the convent by eight, the sun still ablaze. I selected a spot in the bushes where I had a clear view of the convent. I settled in to wait, my backpack held the hurly and the recently acquired Taser. Plus a flask, a blend of coffee and whiskey, I didn't really expect the cat person to show but just in case.

Ten before midnight, I was dozing, the heat still humming in the air, when I saw a hooded figure approach the convent door, carrying a holdall. I watched as the figure opened the holdall and laid a cat on the step, almost delicately and, bizarre as it sounds, laid the carcass with something in the neighbourhood of reverence.

I counted to ten, then with the Taser in my right hand, I came out of the foliage, said,

"Hey."

The figure was startled but didn't run. I kept approaching. The figure reached in their jacket, produced a long knife. For a still moment, we stood like gunfighters, I had the Taser primed and could have dropped the figure right there, but I waited, heard,

"You need to fuck off now, this is not your business."

A woman's voice.

I answered, said,

"Bring it on."

She rushed me and I stepped to the left, brought up my elbow, hit her hard to the side of her head, and she dropped like a stone. I kicked the knife away, bent, and pulled the hood off her head. Looked at the face of a young woman, early twenties, nearly pretty face. The convent door opened, and Therese appeared, said,

"The Guards are on their way."

She went to the young woman, asked me,

"Did you hurt her?"

Really?

The young woman was recovering from my hit, began to sit up, looked at me then Therese, said,

"Cat among the pigeons."

The Guards arrived within minutes, as if they'd been waiting. Maybe they had. The woman was arrested and placed in the back of a police car, the sergeant in charge stared at me and, not with appreciation, snarled,

"How'd you get involved in this, Taylor?"

I told the truth, said,

"I'm a friend of the Mother Superior."

I had to go the station to make a statement, and the atmosphere there was suspicious hostility. The young woman was charged with trespass, public order disturbance, and cruelty to animals. She never spoke, just stood with her head down. As I prepared to finally leave, the young woman looked at me, said,

"Thank you."

Go figure.

Turned out she was twenty-three, named Melly Lee, lived at home with her parents; her father was a doctor, and her mother was a dietician. They had a very grand house by the golf club.

They didn't keep cats.

41

LOCAL ACE VENTURA STRIKES AGAIN

Thus ran the headline on the local paper, detailing my latest exploit.

Jack Taylor, the private detective who saved the swans years ago, helped the Travellers, helped find the perpetrator of attacks on the nuns, champion of the homeless, has yet again solved a case that had baffled the Guards. A series of bizarre incidents at the local convent were solved by Taylor in what has been described as an act of genuine public service. Mr. Taylor was unavailable for comment, but sources close to the man describe him as a legend.

The article went on at some length to praise me own self and had found an old photo that in truth made me look shifty if not downright sinister.

I was in my apartment, drinking a Seven and Seven.

That is 7UP and Seagram's and I had been introduced to it by the writer Craig McDonald. It was smooth and easy on the stomach. A fitting dram for a legend, I thought.

The doorbell went and I debated not answering but what the hell, I had a mellow buzz going, so I should be able for whoever it was.

I opened the door to a middle-aged, well-dressed woman with distress all over her face. She asked in a quiet voice,

"Mr. Taylor?"

I nodded and she said,

"I'm Sheila Lee."

I said nothing and, flustered, she said,

"Melly's mother?"

I asked her in, her shoulders were slumped, the weight of a brutal world.

I made some coffee, went,

"Something stronger?"

She shook her head furiously, said,

"God, no, if I start, I may never stop."

Got that.

I made the coffee and handed her a mug; her hands shook so much, she couldn't hold it. She said,

"Maybe I could have something with a bite after all."

I built her a Seven and Seven, and she held it in both hands, got it down in one tremulous go. Then she sat back, let a breath out, said,

"Phew."

She composed herself, began,

"Mel has always been—"

Pause.

"—different."

She lost her thought for a moment, regrouped, continued,

"She acted out from an early age; we took her to doctors, psychiatrists, the diagnosis was always the same, a personality disorder that could be managed with meds."

I asked,

"Did they work?"

She gave a fleeting smile, not related to humour, said,

"They made her quiet, secretive, she stopped taking them."

I didn't know what she wanted from me, asked,

"What is it you want from me?"

She said,

"Mel refuses to meet with anybody, she's at home under house arrest."

I waited.

"Mel says she'll only talk to one person."

Uh-oh.

But I played, asked,

"Who?"

"You, Mr. Taylor."

Fuck.

I asked,

"Why?"

She shook her head, said,

"I don't know. She read about you in the paper and said you were an outlaw."

I had no reply to this, well, none that bordered on sanity. She leant toward me, the Seagram's giving colour to her face, pleaded,

"Will you?"

I really didn't want to, no good could come of it.

"I'll see her."

How to dress to meet a cat killer?

Black 501s, Docs, off-white T-shirt. I checked myself in the mirror, I looked like a retired dockhand. That should work, no chance I was going to dazzle her with my wardrobe. It was arranged I'd meet her at her home, her bail stipulated she live there until a trial date had been arranged.

The house was impressive, built like the old Georgian houses in Dublin. Neat gardens, recent white paint on the exterior. A house that was cared for.

I rang the bell and Mrs. Lee answered. She was even more nervous than before. She reeked of booze, that sweet cloying breath you think you can cover.

You can't.

She said,

"Mel is in the conservatory at the back; would you like a drink?"

Conservatory!

I passed on the drink, headed down the long hall, the door was open. Mel was sitting in a hard chair, dressed in a white tracksuit, her hair pulled back in one of those severe buns that seem painful. No makeup; she looked about seventeen. She could have been pretty but a twist to her mouth indicated a meanness of spirit. She indicated I should sit opposite her. I smelled patchouli oil, was instantly transported to the sixties and that lost time in every sense. A time that the dream of being a guard was my obsession.

I said,

"You wanted to see me."

She smiled, displaying white, even teeth.

"We're alike."

I gave her a smile back, said,

"I don't have the tendency to kill cats."

She considered that then shot back,

"You kill people, I googled you."

Touché.

Her eyes glittered with a malignant glee, she stood up, asked,

"How about we do some shots?"

I felt the urge to laugh, not from humour but a kind of resigned despair. I asked,

"Why did you want to see me?"

She did a small twirl, light on her feet.

"We could light up this whole town."

Jesus.

I asked,

"Why did you kill the cats?"

She sat down again, said,

"I hate cats, I hate nuns, seemed fitting to bring them together."

She was so far out-there, sanity wasn't even in the neighbourhood.

I asked,

"What now?"

She seemed on the edge of blurting something, but a cloud passed over her face and she shut down.

"I'm bored with you."

I tried,

"Here is my number; when you next feel a wave of action approaching, call me."

I handed her a small white card with my number on it. As I turned to leave, she tore it into pieces, said,

"This is me shredding your old, useless life."

She was on her feet, snarling, spat,

"You're throwing me under the bus."

I said,

"Get the number 46, it's always on time."

Outside, her mother was waiting.

"What should we do?"

I could have trotted out some lazy ideas, but there is a time when a harsh truth is the only path. I said,

"Lock her up."

Two days later, Mel Lee
    Threw herself
    Under a bus.
    It was
    The 46
    And it was on time.

42

I was standing on the new pathway of the Salmon Weir Bridge. It was an impressive build. The day was brightening, and I sat on one of the new benches.

Sure enough, I didn't have solitude for long. In Galway, you rarely do.

A priest.

Father Richard. He asked,

"May I join you?"

I nodded, he sat maybe a bit too close.

He was quiet for a while then,

"You'll have heard the Edge is in disarray, and word is you helped take the main player off the board."

I gave him the look, the one that warns, *mind your fucking step.*

He continued,

"Since the very beginnings of this city, the Edge have been right alongside the growth. And word is, a new cabal is already forming."

"You're telling me this why?"

He stretched his legs, took a deep breath.

"You have been an unlikely aid to the church and in light of that, I have been tasked to warn you, the new Edge will not—"

He paused, searching for a suitable term, found,

"—tolerate any interference from you."

I smiled at him, asked,

"Living on the edge—you know the term?"

He did. I stood up, stretched my own self, leaned in close to him, near whispered,

"The edge? It's where I shine."

43

Time back, I was in Tonery's, one of the few surviving pubs in Bohermore.

An elderly man known as Sean Ban (white John) had worked on the railways with my dad. I remember as a child he'd slip me a half crown, whisper,

"Spend it foolishly."

I did.

I was working on a second pint when he approached, asked,

"A quiet word, young Taylor?"

Young!

God bless his eyesight.

We moved to one of the window snugs and I bought him, as he termed it, a small Paddy. No, not a tiny Irishman, but the old-fashioned whiskey. He'd been horrified when the barman asked if he wanted it on ice. He near spat,

"You are heathen."

Then we toasted with sláinte and he leaned in close to me; he smelled of that Clan pipe tobacco, a comforting aroma reminiscent of an imaginary comfortable childhood. He said,

"I had to borrow two hundred quid from a moneylender, the bills keep piling up, it's warmth or food."

Indeed.

He continued,

"The interest was crazy, and I now have to give the bollix a thousand euro before Friday."

I saved him the shame of asking, said,

"Mind my pint."

And within ten minutes I was back with a fat envelope, handed it over, said,

"There's a little extra for the gas bills."

He had tears in his eyes, blame the Paddy. He reached in his pea jacket, passed over a bundle, said,

"It's the old-style model but it works grand, I kept it oiled and cleaned in case I had need of other means to deal with the moneylender."

I could tell from the shape it was the classic revolver. He said,

"It has six in the chamber, the pull on the hammer is a little strained so you need to lean on it."

Leaning I can do. . . .

He looked at me, said,

"That quare profession you're in, you need all the help available."

Quare? The PC gang would have a riot over that.

He insisted on standing me a drink and I said,

"Well, the Paddy seems to be slipping down nicely."

Later, much later, we parted outside the pub, he said,

"God bless you, young Taylor, I'll repay you."

He wouldn't, because men of his calibre never get clear, more's the Irish pity.

He added,

"Your Pa loved you."

Payment enough.

I had thought a lot about the man who wanted me to kill him.

Peter Bird and the ten thousand euro.

He had said,

"I'm a betting man and I bet you will come through for me."

It was the eve of his birthday; tomorrow was D-day.

I was examining the revolver Sean had given me. It was in fine condition and, true enough, the hammer snagged a bit, but some oil fixed that. I laid the bullets before me.

Picked one at random and put it in the chamber, gave the cylinder a strong roll, then laid the gun down.

The man liked a bet.

Well, now he had a one-in-six shot, literally.

Trip was finally home.

Went out early, took the dog. The title of the Kate Atkinson book was in my head. I was dressed in my black gear, had the revolver in the back of my jeans, it felt bulky. The gun Gustav had given me was again hidden in the sand near Blackrock.

I got to the house, rang the doorbell, took the gun out, held it by my side, rang the bell.

He opened the door, looking surprised at the early hour, a half-eaten piece of toast in his hand.

I took a step back, raised the gun, said,

"Happy birthday."